CW00349043

Reader Reviews of *Secrets of The Italian Gardener*

"This is not a long book, but it is **a classic** piece of **well-written, thoughtful** and worthwhile fiction. Despite the lightness of touch some very serious issues are touched upon, and dealt with in a satisfying way. This is the sort of book that people who read a lot of books are happy to recommend."

"... it has really left **a deep and thoughtful impact**. Andrew Crofts' story is a **beautiful** look at what it is like having to view the world changing around you, both personally and globally, and having no real way to affect the outcomes in it. The characters are **complex**, the imagery of scenes **vivid** and **beautiful**, and it allows us to explore the ideas of who, or what, is considered wrong and right. Will the choices of our past and present really represent how we are viewed in the future? Or can the carefully crafted words of a witness to a key moment in history change the outlook for the entire world? I feel my review may not accurately capture **the jewel that this small story is**, and I encourage anyone to read it and discover what the secrets are, both in the gardens and in your own life."

"A **philosophical** yet **unnerving** look at power, tyranny and fear through the eyes of a ghostwriter and a worldly gardener who turns out to be anything but the man he appears."

"**Delightfully unexpected**, this novella is an **excellent** read."

"Robert Harris meets Paulo Coelho in a **thoughtful, intelligent** story."

"The story is quite **fascinating** and the **thoughtful** nature of the prose allows remarkable insight into the greed and corruption which lies at the heart of a fraudulent regime."

"Coelho with cojones ..."

"*Secrets of the Italian Gardener* is an **original, well-written** story, and a thoroughly good read."

"A **fast-paced** political thriller."

"Packed with **drama** and **political intrigue**, the story draws you in from the first page."

WHAT LIES AROUND US

ANDREW CROFTS

Published by RedDoor
www.reddoorpublishing.com

© 2019 Andrew Crofts

ISBN 978-1-910453-70-4

Cover design: Clare Connie Shepherd
www.clareconnieshepherd.com

Typesetting: Westchester Publishing Services

Print managed by Jellyfish Solutions Ltd

This book is dedicated to Susan, who is the real Caroline and much, much more

"That's our job. To tell a really good story about who we are"

– Barack Obama

1

ഇറ

It is possible that since this book's publication you will have heard that I have died in "suspicious circumstances". Obviously I hope that will not be the case, but I believe it is worth taking the risk in order to get this story out there. We are living in strange and unpredictable times and anything that sheds even the dimmest of lights into the dark corners where the people who run the world are now lurking, is worth trying.

The day the first email arrived, Caroline suggested I start a diary, although neither of us had the slightest idea how enormous the story would become. I certainly never imagined that the whole world would be reading it in this form. Nobody knew what was being plotted behind tightly sealed doors at that stage, apart of course from those who were doing the plotting. Even if someone had guessed and had put forward their theory to the public, they would have been dismissed as nothing more than a conspiracy-theorist. There have been so many conspiracy theories floating around in recent years that most of the time most of us give them no credibility at all, however entertaining or intriguing they might seem at first glance. After enjoying them for a few moments we dismiss them either as "propaganda" from vested interests, or "fake news" designed to turn us into "click bait".

That is what makes being a ghostwriter so addictive; being given permission to gradually unpeel the layers of any story, like an artichoke, as you try to get to a truth, winning people's confidence so they tell you things they didn't mean to, following a trail which you hope will eventually make people want to keep reading. You gradually remove those hard outer layers that have become folded around that core of truth, that delicious heart (to stretch the artichoke metaphor).

Those layers of untruth and obfuscation form because everyone has an angle, everyone sees things differently, remembers things differently, or has something to hide from a judgemental media and public or from a political foe who might use information to their advantage. Even in this age of "transparency" there are always hidden things waiting to be revealed. If there weren't there would be no market for the goods that are peddled by "whistle-blowers" or by those old-fashioned creatures of the night, investigative journalists. Everyone wants to achieve different things with the telling of any story. In the end, once all those layers have been discarded, the soft, vulnerable meat of the heart is exposed and a truth emerges to delight those who will be feasting upon it. For those of us who normally choose to travel a naïve path through life, believing the best in people, ignoring the conspiracy mongers, these revelations nearly always come as a shock – but shocks can also sometimes be stimulating and refreshing things to receive.

All I knew was that I had been contacted personally by one of the mightiest beasts from the world of the business and technology superpowers. Roger Rex's name was right up there with Steve Jobs, Bill Gates, Mark Zuckerberg and Elon Musk; a modern-day witch doctor who was believed to not only be able to see into the future but to be able to shape it too; a magician for our times. And instead of a fire-breathing dragon, this sorcerer had his billions to give credibility to the rumours of his magical powers and stupendous brain.

"If that email is actually from him," Caroline said as she neatly scraped food up Maddy's chin and into her already bulging cheeks, wielding the pink plastic spoon like a cutthroat razor, "then you could be about to witness stuff which will become the history of the twenty-first century. You should record it all for posterity. Keep a diary of everything that happens. You never know – it could turn out to be Maddy's inheritance."

Maddy gave a squawk of excitement at the sound of her own name, snapping open her mouth for more food.

I was aware that the email could have been a hoax.

I mean, what were the chances that one of the half dozen richest people on the planet had actually sat down and written a note directly to me? But there was no reason not to accept it at face value, at least until it proved to be something else. The message was simple: *I am going to be in London next week and I would really like to discuss a possible project. Could we meet for lunch? I will be staying at the Four Seasons.*

Even if it came to no more than a lunch with Roger Rex at the Four Seasons it would be an adventure worth having. *I would love to,* I emailed back, *just let me know where and when you would like to meet.*

"Do you like Chinese?" he asked as he clumsily enveloped my hand in his in the foyer of the hotel a few days later, pumping it energetically, holding on a few seconds longer than I expected as if to compensate for not making more than a flicker of eye contact. The walls around us were the colour of blood, as were the rims of his over-sized glasses. His outfit, right down to his backpack and trainers, was black.

"Absolutely." I enthused.

"Great, I've booked a table up the road. Do you mind walking?"

Our destination proved to be China Tang, a dark, lush restaurant in the bowels of the Dorchester Hotel, no more than five minutes' walk at a billionaire's lanky gallop. He talked every step of the way, stirring up a tsunami of enthusiasm for his experiences thus far in London, and for every passing thing that caught his attention – the trees in Hyde Park, the double-decker buses in Park Lane, my blue suede shoes – allowing me a welcome chance to catch my breath as I tried to keep up and pretend I always walked at this speed. He seemed genuinely excited by every sight, sound and smell, simultaneously throwing out opinions and thoughts about news items which had reached him through the media that morning or facts he had recently learned and was eager to share. He had arrived in England via Scandinavia and as we weaved our way through the Dorchester's lavishly furnished and gilded "Promenade", he managed to give me a quick verbal tour of every country he had been to, exclaiming repeatedly at the wonders of their smooth-working democracies. He was convinced he had "seen the future" and that "it works". He dived downstairs to the restaurant, two steps at a time, talking over his shoulder with every bound.

"I love your work, Andrew," he said once the complications of the menu had been ironed out and the staff had quietly withdrawn to prepare the meal as ordered and attend to other customers. "Particularly the human interest stories; ordinary people battling against the odds ..."

"Really?" I said. "You've read my work?"

"Of course," he seemed shocked by the suggestion that he might have come to a meeting unprepared. Leaning down beside his chair he dipped his hand into his backpack, which he had refused to relinquish to the staff at reception, producing *Secrets of the Italian Gardener* with a flourish, making the gold inlay of the cover glitter in the subdued restaurant lights. "Fantastic story. And short too. I like a book I can read in one flight." He paused for a moment before adding awkwardly, "my condolences on your loss by the way."

"Thank you."

The social niceties apparently now out of the way he reverted to monologue-mode. I wished I was recording him because I wanted to remember everything he was saying so that I could relay it to Caroline once I was home, but our relationship had not yet reached a point where I could whip out a Dictaphone or a notepad. At this stage it was just a casual lunch and I still had no idea why he wanted to meet me. Everything he said was interesting. There was too much of it for me to hope to remember more than a few main themes; too many ideas, too many digressions, too many extraordinary pieces of information and exciting predictions, all sparkling with the most dazzling name-drops in the world – Clinton, Obama, Gates, Mandela, Zuckerberg, Bezos, Soros, Clooney, Swift, de Niro and Streep – delivered with no apparent self-awareness, simply reporting something interesting they had said to him or done. He had no need to boast about who he knew, it just so happened that many of the people he talked to in the course of his average days were world famous. I wasn't even sure that he realised how famous they were, or cared. He asked my views on every subject that he raised but never gave me enough time to answer before chasing off after a new train of thought. With each new dish that was brought to the table his monologue would take a radical swerve, his attention distracted by the look of the food, the aromas and the tastes.

"Oh my God, you have to try this! This is fantastic. This is the best in the world. Let's order more!"

* * *

Being in his company was exhilarating, comical and enthralling. I tried to remember to eat as well as memorise everything he was saying. I wanted a chance to learn everything I could from this encounter before he disappeared out of my life as abruptly as he had entered. The mental effort was exhausting, leaving me no space to follow any agenda of my own, and it wasn't until we were finishing our desserts that I realised he had still said nothing about why he had asked to meet me.

"So," I grabbed a fleeting opportunity to interrupt his flow, "are you thinking of writing a book?"

"Sure," he said, apparently surprised by the question, "sure, sure, but not yet."

"Not yet?" I probably wasn't able to hide my disappointment. My enthusiasm for the prospect of working with him had been growing throughout the meal.

"There's something completely different that we need to talk about. How much interference are you willing to put up with?"

"I'm sorry?"

"If we were to commission a book but we had very strong ideas about what should or shouldn't be in it, would you mind being told and having to re-write and edit a great deal?"

"Usually I suggest that I write the first draft as I think it should be," I replied, "but ultimately it is the author's story, so they can make whatever changes they want. When you say 'we' would have very strong ideas ... ?"

"There are a few people interested in the outcome of this book. It could have huge global impact. Absolutely huge."

"It's better if there is one person I am ultimately answerable too. If everyone is allowed to have an opinion ..."

"Oh yes, of course; that would be me. No committees. That would be the worst. So you won't be offended if you are asked to keep re-writing and changing things?"

"I'm very hard to offend," I assured him. "As long as I'm being paid for my time ..."

"Money is not an issue," he brushed my comment aside as a waitress removed our plates, neatly scraped the crumbs from the cloth with a small silver implement and took our orders for double espressos.

"Can you give me an idea what you mean by 'global impact'?"

"Not yet, no. Not until you've talked to the lawyers. You would be great for this job, really great. Your books made me cry. You've done celebrity books too, right?"

"Yes, a few."

"It's important not to be star struck."

I remembered reading that he had been buying up film studios and television networks, corralling creative talent so that he could control the creation of the content he needed for streaming services into smartphones and social media. Were these the sort of stars he was talking about? I felt my heart thump a little faster – surely everyone's star struck about somebody.

"Can you tell me anything about the story at all?"

"No," he shook his head and gave a sharp bark of laughter which made several heads turn in our direction. "Lawyers. You'll have to sign away your life before we can tell you anything. Do you have an agent? Is there someone we have to talk to?"

"We can go through an agent if you like," I said, "there are a few who I use for different projects. Or you can just deal with me."

"We would prefer that, if you don't mind. If there is an agent involved then that is one more person who has to know at least some of the details of the project, one more person who might leak, one more stage in the process, slowing things down. This is really great coffee! Such a great aroma." He held the tiny cup close to his nostrils and inhaled deeply, closing his eyes in apparent ecstasy. "We will want to pay you an outright fee so that we own the copyright completely. Your name would be visible nowhere. Would that be a problem?"

"Absolutely not."

"This is great, really great. It's going to be so great!" he rocked happily back in his chair, clapping loudly, his huge hands flapping like a seal's flippers. "I'll get the lawyers to contact you. We are going to make history."

2

୫୦୦ଓ

The lawyers seemed surprised that I was on my own when I arrived at the appointed time the following week in their glassy offices in Holborn.

"Are we expecting your representative to join us?" the lead lawyer asked as we sat round the shiny table amidst a sea of empty leather armchairs.

"No. I don't have a representative. Do I need one?"

"Not as long as you feel comfortable," she smiled and slid a three-page document across the table. "Can we start with you signing this non-disclosure? Then we can talk more openly. Please read it. Take your time."

I forced myself to read through every line as they waited in silence, even though it seemed like standard stuff. I never did talk about any of my clients anyway, so it wasn't asking me to agree to anything difficult. I scribbled a signature and skidded it back across the table into her lap.

"Thank you," she said as she retrieved it. No smile this

time as she glanced at the signature before slipping the papers into a black leather folder, apparently satisfied. "Are you familiar with an actress called Jo-Jo Win?"

"Yes, of course."

"This is a commission to ghostwrite a book for her."

"An autobiography?"

Why would Roger Rex be so interested in commissioning a book on behalf of a Hollywood actress, unless it was for the obvious romantic reasons? He hadn't seemed like the sort of man who would allow such a superficial matter as sex to distract him from the hundreds of world-changing projects racing around in his head, but then many beautiful women through history have been known to turn great men's brains to mush. Arthur Miller and Marilyn Monroe for instance, or Lord and Lady Macbeth.

"Partly autobiography, but also a book of her philosophies and beliefs; her family history. It would be a major undertaking. You would need to be prepared to travel to the West Coast for an extended period."

"Why do they want an English writer?"

"They think we're smarter," she allowed herself a smirk; "It's the accent. And of course they've heard of Shakespeare, Dickens, Ian Fleming, J K Rowling."

"What is Roger Rex's interest in Jo-Jo Win?"

"Just a friend and business associate," she waved aside the question while holding my eyes with hers, daring me to pursue that impudent line of questioning. "Did you and Roger talk money?"

"No. He said it would not be a problem."

She opened her leather folder and glanced at something inside. "We suggest a million dollars in instalments."

I tried not to allow any untoward gurgling noises to escape me as I replied. "I would need business class expenses if I am travelling outside the UK."

"That wouldn't be a problem. Your travel and accommodation would be taken care of."

"I would need to see the schedule for the payments ..."

She had slid another piece of paper across from her folder before I had time to finish the request. It suggested that I should be paid a quarter in advance, a quarter on acceptance of a first draft, a quarter on acceptance of the final draft and a quarter on first publication. Probably, if I had brought an agent or lawyer with me, I could have improved the offer, but it would have seemed churlish to even try to haggle in the face of such apparent generosity.

"That would be acceptable," I said, because it was – more than.

"Good," she nodded to one of her juniors who opened a leather folder identical to hers, which was sitting on the table in front of him, and passed her three copies of a thick contract. "We will need you to sign these. You will need to read through them."

"Can I take them away to study?"

"No. We would not want these papers to leave the building. Would you like another coffee?"

* * *

The lawyer/agent that I did not have with me would certainly not have let me sign there and then. There would have been weeks of careful reading, followed by further weeks of back and forth and arguments over sub-clauses. The idea of such delays and so much attention to detail made me feel nauseous, so I accepted the pot of coffee and read them as quickly as I could manage while still giving the impression of being professional and thorough. I signed them without asking questions, hoping that I was not making any serious errors of judgement and still feeling nauseous from the fear that I might have fallen into some cleverly laid, lawyerly trap. The thought that I might simply be being greedy in wanting to get the deal signed quickly, or lazy for not wanting to think more deeply about the details of the deal than I had to, also made me feel guilty. The thought of a million dollars and a trip to California, however, more than compensated.

3

⊰ ⊱

"You can't breathe a word to a single living soul, ever," I told Caroline that evening once Maddy was safely asleep and we were downstairs in the kitchen, chopping vegetables, "otherwise the lawyers will throw away the key and I will never see the outside world again and Maddy will have a convict for a father."

"Jesus," she laughed, "lighten up. I promise never to tell anyone your sordid little secret."

"It's Jo-Jo Win."

"You're kidding! Your little guilty pleasure?"

"What do you mean?"

"You fancy her."

"No I don't!" I protested, aware that the colour was rising in my cheeks.

"Of course you do, everyone does. That's why she's a star."

"She's not that great," I muttered feebly.

"You admitted you fancied her when we were having supper with the others!"

"That was a dinner party game," I protested, "everyone had to name someone they would choose if their partner gave them permission. I was drunk! You chose someone too!"

I wished I could remember who it was Caroline had named that evening, I felt woefully under-prepared for this discussion.

"You couldn't take your eyes off her when she was rushing around zapping the baddies and saving the world in that video game movie thing."

"Well, maybe a bit. But that's all CGI. I might as well have fancied Jessica Rabbit or Marge Simpson."

She grinned triumphantly at my half-hearted protests. "It's all right, I don't mind. You're entitled to a little crush now and then. You have my permission to go write a book with the love of your life."

"Suddenly she's gone from my 'little guilty pleasure' to the 'love of my life'?"

She chewed thoughtfully on a carrot, saying nothing, peering down her nose at me with narrowed eyes, her head tilted back, like I was a specimen on a laboratory bench.

"You're the love of my life," I mumbled, scraping the vegetables into the wok.

"I know," she said, pecking me on the cheek, taking a swig of wine and refilling her glass. "Just don't forget it when you're locked in Action Woman's boudoir, listening to her pouring out all her secrets. So, what's the connection to Roger Rex?"

"I don't know. Maybe she's his guilty pleasure as well."

"Let's Google them together and see what comes up."

"Maybe, given the number of lawyers standing guard, not such a good idea to keep a diary after all," I said as she came back in with her laptop.

"Are you kidding? Definitely keep a diary. Just hide it really well."

She became lost to surfing for a few minutes. "He doesn't seem to have any sort of love interests at all. There are pictures of him standing next to virtually every famous woman in the world but at no stage is he touching any of them, not even an arm round the waist for the benefit of the photographer. He never seems to be making eye contact with anyone either. I suppose he's another one on the spectrum, is he?"

I thought about it for a moment. "Yes, probably."

"Most of these technology billionaires are."

"Maybe he's gay," I said, doubtfully. Now I thought about it I hadn't picked up any sexual vibes from the man at all during our short time together.

"No sign of anything in that department either. I guess he's channelled all his testosterone into the work."

"So, he's not doing this to woo her then?"

"Well, there are no pictures or stories of them together," she said eventually, "apart from a few mutual business interests. She seems to be happily married to a blond actor hunk called Charlie Huck. Two beautiful blonde kids, loves nothing more than cooking family meals and reading them bed-time stories, blah, blah, blah."

"If that's what they're saying online they'll probably announce their divorce tomorrow."

"She really is big news in the States," Caroline continued to read, her curiosity now piqued. "I didn't realise. Millions of teen fan followers because of the video games and she's a feminist icon to boot. She and her family have launched a reality TV show – like we need another. She's clever too. Seems to be a big investor in Silicon Valley start-ups. Most of them really successful. Maybe that's the connection to your friend. Yes!" she exclaimed triumphantly, "he owns the production company making her reality show."

"Maybe that's why they're paying me the big bucks," I said, casually refilling my wine glass.

"How big?"

"A million dollars," I said, unable to suppress the accompanying grin. "Signed the contract today."

"Fucking hell. Don't they realise you would have done it for a quarter of that?"

"Maybe even less, given she's my guilty little pleasure."

"I wonder why they're willing to pay so much."

"Maybe they expect her to make my life very difficult indeed."

"There is a suggestion of control freakery going on

here," Caroline agreed as she continued to read, "but still, that's a scary amount of money for one book."

"Assuming I make it all the way to the end of the project."

"Who's the publisher?"

"Apparently they haven't got one. I think they are thinking of self-publishing. That would fit with the control-freakery aspect. I can't imagine that she or Roger Rex would fancy handing ninety per cent of the book's earnings to Penguin or Simon and Schuster."

"I should think they would be able to get a big enough advance to make that irrelevant," Caroline was now thinking like a publisher.

"They would still have to hand over at least some of the control for the look of the book."

"Still don't quite see why Roger Rex would be so interested."

"He seems to find just about everything fascinating," I said, remembering his enthusiasm for everything from London pigeons to the aroma of a cup of espresso, "maybe he wants to be a book publisher as well as a tech billionaire, film studio owner and whatever else he is."

"It just seems to me there must be some other reason why this is being handled like it is more than your usual film star autobiography. He didn't get to be a billionaire by handing out a million dollars on a whim. Why would intelligent, hard nosed business people be willing to hand over so much money without any sort of fight?"

"Who says I didn't put up a fight?"

She raised a knowing eyebrow to indicate that we both knew the answer was too obvious for her to bother wasting her breath explaining, and returned to her on-screen researches. I turned my attention to the wok.

"She's got an interesting family history; Mexican father, Chinese mother, Liberal Arts degree from New York, post-grad business degree from Harvard. Seems you have good taste in women."

"Undoubtedly," I raised my glass to her but she didn't notice, her eyes too busy flickering through the material she was unearthing, instantly absorbed by the tempting trail of clues opening up before her.

"Wow, she really is impressive."

I went back to stirring the vegetables, relieved that the project had caught her imagination and was therefore more likely to receive her stamp of approval. It always made me uneasy if I told her about some new project and she showed her doubts about it by wrinkling her nose in a way which was simultaneously pretty and disquieting. The rumbles of excitement I had previously been experiencing in the depths of my stomach at the thought of the events that might be about to unfold were now deliciously heightened and threatening to erupt in an uncontrolled burst of joy. I risked enhancing them further with a large mouthful of wine, basking happily in the warmth of the sizzling wok. I felt Caroline's arms sliding round my middle and she leaned round to kiss me on the cheek.

"Well done," she whispered. "I am truly impressed."

There had been so many years during which I had never believed that it would be possible to feel this level of elation ever again.

4

෨උෂ

Roger Rex had allocated me what seemed to be a handler, or maybe a "minder" would have been a better description. Or even a "fixer". She was called Julia and she was waiting for me at the arrivals gate at San Francisco Airport with a sign bearing my name, well at least part of it – "Andy".

We had already spoken. She had phoned me the moment the plane taxied to a halt to introduce herself, so I had no difficulty in recognising her beaming smile of welcome amongst the many waiting relatives and taxi drivers. It was not the sort of smile you could easily miss; radiating the kind of general goodwill that many of us would like to believe might be hiding in our souls, waiting for permission to burst forth.

In Roger's world, I was to discover, people didn't have job titles for fear that they might prove to be limiting. If Julia had worked in a different corporate culture I think she would have been designated a "PA", or maybe a "PR executive". She didn't, however, need a title to win my total confidence. Her competence was obvious from the moment she gripped my hand with the strength of an athlete and a beaming "Hi Andy", and led me clear of the crowds to a waiting car and driver. The car was so new and shiny it looked like it had just slid off a showroom carpet for the first time. The most grown-up purchase Caroline and I had ever indulged in was a nearly new estate car when Maddy was born. It had seemed outrageously luxurious after the few sad wrecks we had owned previously. The smooth, almost silent electronic cocoon that I was now being ushered into, however, was something from an entirely different time and dimension. It was hardly like being in a car at all, more like floating into the future, apparently powered by just the computer screen which was integrated into the dashboard.

"What is this car?" I asked, shocking myself that I would even ask such a question. I had never before felt the slightest murmur of interest regarding any vehicle.

"It's a Tesla," Julia told me. "Do you know Elon?"

"Elon Musk?" Did she assume anyone who knew Roger would know Elon? "I know who he is. I read his biography. I watch his rockets go into space."

"Well, there you go," she beamed. "Elon and Roger are very close. Every time Elon brings out a new model he sends one over for Roger to try. They are such great cars. John loves to drive them. Right, John?"

"Sure do," John the driver agreed. His polo shirt was so brilliantly white and so neatly pressed it gave the impression he was uniformed. "They are great to drive." His wrap-around dark glasses and ear piece made him look like a man with skills in close protection. Between the two of them, and the car, I felt I was in extremely safe hands, cocooned from all outside interference. It was a comforting feeling after a long flight and delivery into an alien environment.

"Okay," Julia continued, consulting the screen of her phone, "what we thought we would do, if it is okay with you, Andy, is take you to the house. Jo-Jo is filming today but hopefully you will be able to get a little face-time, just to say 'hi', and we will settle you into your room, which is beautiful. It is actually a cottage, with its own pool, so you can have private time; I think you will be very comfortable. You can relax after your flight and then we will introduce you to a few people in the family and give you a little orientation. You have my number now and you can call me whenever you need anything or you need to go anywhere and John and I will be at your disposal twenty-four-seven. Any interviews you want to do, or if you just want to go shopping or get a meal, or sight-seeing, just let me know, okay? Roger wants you to feel completely at home, so that you can concentrate on your work. Are there any questions you might have at this stage?"

"That all sounds great," I couldn't think of a single question since I couldn't even begin to imagine the shape that the coming days were going to take on. Was Jo-Jo Win actually going to be able to spare me the time I needed or was I going to have to get all the information from other places? To know that I could pass all my needs on to Julia was as comforting as the hum of the expensive electric car. I felt my eyes closing involuntarily. Both Julia and John were too discreet to interrupt my abrupt descent into sleep, both of them concentrating on their screens. Everything, I felt sure, was going to be taken care of. I could safely switch off my internal travel alert system. I had arrived.

* * *

When I awoke we had been driving for about an hour and I didn't feel any less tired. If anything I felt even worse than when I was woken up by the stewardess on the plane. We seemed to have reached our destination in Los Altos Hills. Automatic gates were opening in high walls to let us into an estate which had been laid out in the style of a vineyard from the old world. It reminded me of the times Caroline and I had spent, before we became parents the first time, driving around Provence and Tuscany in search of cheap accommodation and cheap wine. The walls were pale brown stone and the roofs were covered in thick terracotta tiles. The grounds were planted out with a mixture of tropical and Mediterranean foliage, tranquil as an Italian hilltop village at siesta time and groomed as immaculately as the grounds of a Bel Air hotel.

The car slid between the buildings on cleanly swept brick paths that wound through palms and bougainvillea. The brushing of the leaves against the windows was the loudest sound until we emerged into something akin to a village square, which was shockingly hectic with the bustle and paraphernalia of film crews. Julia phoned someone and announced our arrival.

"Okay," she said, "let's go find Jo-Jo. She's really looking forward to finally meeting you. She's a huge fan of your work."

I dismissed that last comment as American good manners and, from the disconnected look in the film star's eyes as Julia introduced us, I was pretty sure that she had no idea who I was or why I was there. I decided to let Julia handle any possible embarrassment that might be heading our way.

"It's the writer Roger was telling you about."

"Oh, sure, yeah," her eyes were still far away but her light fingers enfolded mine firmly and she sounded genuine as she said, "I read your book; about the Italian Gardener. Loved it." The soft touch of her skin sent a small electric shock through me, a feeling I remembered from the first time Caroline had linked her arm through mine, leaning her head against my shoulder as we walked home from our first proper date. With those small movements Caroline had fulfilled all my hopes and allowed me to dream foolish, exciting dreams of how the future might unfold.

"Thank you," I said, too dizzy from the electric current to be able to think of anything else to say. There was a light, clean scent of jasmine surrounding her.

Even if she was just being polite the fact that she even remembered half the title of my most recent book was awe inspiring. As I grew used to the shock of being in her presence I began to take in just how beautiful she was, although a little older perhaps than in my film-fan memory, and much smaller and more delicate than I had imagined from seeing her on the big screen in the mighty close-ups which emphasised the perfect symmetry of every feature on her face. The most striking thing was her charisma. It's always hard to define star-quality, but impossible to miss it when it comes along. I found myself ridiculously tongue-tied, but she was obviously entirely used to people staring at her with their mouths hanging open and no sensible words coming out. I was relieved that Caroline was not there to witness my descent into slack-jawed fandom. She would have been able to taunt me with an imitation of my own blushing inarticulacy for the rest of my life.

"You have to meet Chuck," Jo-Jo said, still holding my hand and guiding me through the crowd of technicians to a table which was set up with coffee and water, where her blond, tanned husband sat in the sun with two small blonde, tanned children on his lap. "Chuck, this is Andy. He wrote that great book Roger gave us to read."

Chuck shook my hand vigorously and cracked the

whitest grin I had ever been blessed to bask in. "Great to meet you. Loved the book. So sorry for your loss. Really looking forward to spending time with you."

To avoid being dislodged by his movements the kids both put their arms around his neck, clinging on like baby monkeys, staring up at me through velvety lashes with their mother's chocolate coloured, oval eyes. I surrendered my travel weary body and mind into the warm bath of the family's gleaming Californian good-will. No wonder their reality show was proving to be such a hit.

"Listen, Andy," I realised Jo-Jo was talking to me again, her fingers now resting conspiratorially on my arm, and I tried to pull my thoughts together, "we're going to be a few hours finishing up here. I'm going to suggest that Julia settles you into your guest house; you have a rest, and then maybe you should meet up with my mom and dad. They are really looking forward to meeting you. Mom will make you some dinner."

"Jo-Jo's mom is a great cook," Chuck assured me.

"You like Chinese?" Jo-Jo asked, already steering me back towards Julia's care, nodding to someone else who looked like she might be a personal assistant, who was try-ing to capture her attention, as if to assure them she would be finished with me and getting to them within a few seconds.

"Sure," I said.

"Great. That's great, and tomorrow we will spend some

time together and get to know one another properly. I am so looking forward to getting to know you."

Then she was gone, swallowed by a crowd of people far taller than her, and Julia was guiding me off into the gardens to the cottage where my luggage and a steaming rainforest shower were awaiting me.

5

I had dozed off in a pile of white cushions on a sofa overlooking the pool outside my cottage, having thoroughly explored each room and found it fully equipped with everything I could need to exist over the coming days, including a fully stocked bar and a fridge packed with fresh groceries, when I was woken by a voice calling my name. I was shocked to find that the sky had become dark and the foliage around the pool was now lit from below like a theatre set. An elderly man with a dark moustache and laugh lines crinkling his eyes poked his head round the corner, smiling at me pleasantly.

"Are you Andrew?"

"Yes," I struggled to my feet and shook his hand, it was cool and dry.

"Hi. I'm Martin. I've been sent to fetch you for some dinner. Are you hungry?"

"Yes, sure." I actually wasn't sure, but I was going to

have to get my stomach back into some sort of routine in the new time zone.

"That's good. My wife has prepared a feast for you."

"You must be ..."

"I'm sorry, yes; I am Jo-Jo's father. Martin."

I knew a few facts from googling. I knew that he was Dr Martin Win and that he was of Mexican descent, his grandparents having crossed the border after the outbreak of the Mexican Revolution in 1910. On the internet the fact that he was the father of a film star had eclipsed the fact that he had won a great many international awards for his humanitarian and medical work, both in the poorer areas of big American cities and in the developing world. He had written a number of books and was a visiting professor at nearby Stanford University. All this dry, biographical detail was out there, available for anyone who chose to drill down beneath the stuff about his daughter in search of it. I also knew that his wife, Lillian, the daughter of Chinese immigrants who had arrived in San Francisco after the Second World War, had been working as a hospital midwife for more than forty years.

* * *

The meal was already steaming and sizzling on the top of the stove as Martin and I came into their house, a short walk from my guest cottage, but Lillian took the time to give me a firm hug and settle me with a drink, as her husband took over the task of agitating the food until she was ready to return and serve it up. She was exactly the sort of practical, no-nonsense woman you would want looking after you if you were about to spend a good many hours in labour and she smelled as good as her daughter.

"You must be very proud of Jo-Jo," I said once Lillian had loaded my plate to her satisfaction and we were all eating.

"We wanted her to be a doctor," Lillian said. "To carry on Martin's work."

"Lillian was one of those 'Tiger Mothers' you read about," Martin said, his eyes glancing furtively at his wife as if expecting a scolding. "Still is, come to that."

"Her father would have let her get away with everything," Lillian waved her chopsticks at her husband; "someone had to make sure she worked hard."

Martin winked at me. "See what I mean?"

"But maybe she can achieve more good this way," Lillian continued, as if he hadn't spoken. "Roger Rex tells me that if she had been a doctor she wouldn't have had 'a platform'. Everything now is about 'platforms' and about 'building a following'. Maybe this way is better than being an obscure doctor saving lives in some African village no one has ever heard of."

Martin now appeared not to be listening, concentrating contentedly on his food. I suspected he had heard this monologue before.

"Win is an unusual Mexican name," I changed the subject.

"It is my family name," Lillian said. "Martin had a stupid Spanish name, but Win is a good word in the American mind. So we decided to use my name. If you have a Spanish name you always sound like an immigrant. You need a good American name. Everyone wants to 'win', no? Roger Rex agrees with me on that at least."

"Obama didn't do too badly with an immigrant's name," Martin ventured with a hint of mischief in his eyes.

"Have you read that book Obama wrote?" Lillian asked me. "*Dreams from My Father*?"

"Yes, I have."

"That is what Jo-Jo's book should be like. That is what you need to write, Andrew. A beautiful book. Beautiful writing, inspiring ideas and thoughts. That is what Roger Rex needs for building this platform."

"Don't tell him how to write the book, Lillian," Martin said, "he will write it from the heart. He's a professional."

"He needs to know what is required," Lillian chewed enthusiastically as she warmed to her subject. "He has to understand his client's brief."

"We know you will do a great job," Martin assured me, "we've read a lot of your work."

"Roger Rex says you are the best in the world," Lillian announced, oblivious to the blush such a lack of irony was bringing to my cheeks, or perhaps she was simply unbothered by such things as modesty. I had never before been in receipt of so much flattery from so many people in such a short time.

"My wife puts a lot of store by the pronouncements of Roger Rex," Martin said.

"He's a very clever man. He has built one of the biggest companies in the world – biggest in all history. Billions and billions of dollars. He must know something."

"Indeed," Martin laughed. "A great man of his moment."

"You eat very slowly," Lillian gestured accusingly at my still heaped plate. "Would you like something different?"

"Leave him alone, Lillian," Martin laughed. "He's enjoying a leisurely meal. Not everyone eats at the same speed as you."

"I like to do everything fast," she admitted, "You achieve more that way. There is always so much to do every day. Always so little time."

"Not only Win by name, you see," Martin said. She seemed entirely unaware of the look of intense love that her husband gave her as she ladled more food onto both their plates.

"You need to talk to us first," Lillian told me once she was eating again. "We can tell you everything you need so that you know what questions to ask Jo-Jo."

"Lillian, the poor guy has only just stepped off the plane."

"Come for breakfast in the morning and bring your recording machine. You use a recording machine?"

"Yes," I laughed, unsure how to respond to such direct orders, "I use a recording machine."

"Good. Bring it. I'll make you breakfast. I've taken two days off work. I have a lot to say."

"I'm sure Andrew doesn't doubt that, my dear."

"Oh, you be quiet, old man. I know what he needs to know."

"You don't know what has already been planned for him tomorrow. He might be seeing Roger or Jo-Jo and Chuck ..."

"Chuck?" her chopsticks froze in mid-air, "what's the point in him talking to Chuck?"

"Chuck is her husband," Martin spoke quietly, "and the father of her children. He's a big part of her story. The marriage is important."

"I'll tell you all you need to know about the marriage and the kids," Lillian told me. "Never mind about Chuck. Leave him to do his surfing."

Martin caught my eye and shook his head conspiratorially, as if warning me not to pursue that particular line of conversation.

That night, back in the cottage and unable to sleep, I went on to YouTube and put in Jo-Jo's name. Hundreds of clips from the reality show immediately sprung up, mostly set in the big open-plan kitchen of their home. The clips had all been viewed tens of millions of times. After them came clips from her movies, mostly showing her fighting multiple baddies with a mixture of superhuman athleticism and double-handed firepower, and after that came a variety of interviews, which she had obviously been contracted to do in order to promote the films. In all of them the interviewers seemed to be struck almost inarticulate with adoration.

6

ॐ

When my phone next woke me I had no idea what time of the day it was. I lay very still, trying to concentrate and work it out. On the ceiling above the bed the reflections of the morning sun were bouncing off the pool. When my eyes had focused enough to see the screen I answered.

"Hi, Andy. It's Julia. Roger would really like to meet with you for breakfast in an hour or so. I'll come pick you up from the cottage."

Back in the Tesla an hour later I was now armed with recorders and notepads, putting myself into "soaking-everything-up" mode.

"I think Lillian is expecting me for breakfast too," I said.

"Isn't she just adorable?" Julia said. "I would give anything for her to be my mom."

"She seems like a strong character."

"Soooo strong. I think you'll find Jo-Jo gives her a lot of credit for everything good that's happened. A lot of credit."

"Martin was lovely too. They obviously make a wonderful couple."

"Such a wonderful couple. Wouldn't anyone just love to have them for parents? He is the nicest man. He won the Nobel Prize."

I was pretty sure that wasn't true but I didn't bother to contradict her. He had won enough prizes to have more than earned an exaggerated reputation.

"Can you let them know that I won't be there for breakfast?"

"Oh they are being fully briefed at every stage. They are so important to this project. Roger wants them to be completely involved, completely on message, completely on-board. He has so much respect for them, for their authenticity. They are amazing people."

* * *

Roger's gangly limbs were stretched out across several giant yellow beanbags in an office made of pale wood and glass, with views out across parkland so immaculate it looked like it had been planted up the night before. He was surrounded by a dozen or so other people, all much younger than him, in similarly relaxed poses. All of them were engrossed in whatever was happening on their laptops and tablets. Some of them wore fully immersive headphones, talking to unseen callers in the same tones they might talk to friends in a coffee shop, at the same time as tapping on keys. Roger waved me down onto an empty beanbag next to him while Julia went in search of food and drink.

"I wanted you to see this," he said. "I want you to know just how much we are supporting this project. All these guys are working full-time on building Jo-Jo's platform, interacting with her followers, making personal connections for her."

"Lillian was telling me about the platform."

"Lillian is a great person," he said as he tapped the keys. It was the first time I had heard an edge of impatience, or perhaps irritation, in his voice, "really great, but she doesn't know what she is talking about when it comes to social media. Such a great mother though. Martin too, such a great father figure. They have both overcome such huge odds to be where they are. Fantastic success stories. We are very close."

He turned his screen towards me and I could see it was filled with messages coming through from places like Facebook, Twitter and WhatsApp, all for Jo-Jo. It took me a moment to realise that the people around me on the floor were the ones typing in the answers in Jo-Jo's name. A lot of it was trivial nonsense; teenage girls asking her about her make-up, mothers of small children asking her what she thought about Ritalin or wives asking what she liked to cook for Chuck when they were alone. But

39

many were far more politically connected, asking her views about women's rights, children's rights, gun rights, immigration issues, racism and sexism. Every question was being treated with the same degree of seriousness and politeness, even the obscene or hate-filled ones. Even the death threats. The replies all sounded personal, like they might actually be coming from her, like she might actually care about the anonymous typist on the other end of the cyber conversation.

"This is what technology has made possible," Roger said. "It is so great! We can connect directly with hundreds of people at once, properly interact with them, not just shake their hands and sign their autograph books; but talk to them like real people. Young people today are very serious minded about a lot of things. So engaged. It's great. Look here." He directed my attention to a thread from someone in Minnesota who went by the name of Rosie-Posie. She was deeply worried about the growing inequality between the top one per cent and the rest of the population. "The rich," she wrote, "just keep getting richer, while more and more people are ending up living on the streets". Whoever was responding as Jo-Jo was engaging fully on the subject, sympathising, agreeing, asking her if she had any ideas what could be done about the problem. I wondered if Rosie-Posie had any idea how rich Jo-Jo was. I guessed everyone sprawled on those bean-bags was safely part of the one per cent she was complaining about.

"There are these ones too," Roger said, tapping on another message from someone calling themselves Alt-Right-All-Right, who was threatening Jo-Jo with all kinds of physical harm, ranting about her mixed race background and how she and her "brat-bastards" should be sent straight back across the Mexican border. "However rude or abusive they are, she responds with understanding and courtesy. There is no way of knowing who they actually are or what sort of troubles they have in their own lives. There is nothing to be gained from confrontation. If they get a polite response from Jo-Jo some of them just might revise their opinions of her, just might see that their behaviour is inappropriate. Always look for the good in everyone, that's the rule."

"There's an actual death threat there," I pointed out.

"Sure. We get a few of them, and rape threats. We log them, just in case they turn out to be serious threats, but usually they too respond well to a polite, personalised response. In most cases they are people who are used to being ignored. They just want to connect, to be heard. Just receiving a personalised response blows their mind. It's great to connect with these people in positive ways. We can make their lives better simply by reaching out."

"Do you think they actually believe that it is Jo-Jo they are talking to?"

"Some of them work out pretty quickly that it isn't. If they challenge us we explain that Jo-Jo sets the tone for everything we say to them. It is a bit like a kid meeting

41

Santa Claus in a department store. Every kid above the age of five or six understands the concept of the real Santa having to deal with the whole world. It's obvious he is going to have to delegate some of the face-to-face contact. Right? The messages are the same whichever Santa you are talking to; goodwill, lots of presents, ho-ho-ho! Right? The kids still go away happy. Right?"

"So it's like getting an autographed photo from a fan club, knowing that the star would never have had the time to sign it themselves – if you stop to think about it – but still loving it? A sort of willing suspension of disbelief."

"Great description! But much more personal than that, much more intimate. Ultimately we will be straight about who they are actually talking to with anyone who challenges us, but most people are happy to go along with the pretence because it feels good."

"Just like Santa."

"Yeah," he grinned. "Just like Santa. Everyone loves the idea of meeting Santa, right? Of actually talking to him. You should spend some time with these guys." He gestured round the cushions and waved vaguely in the direction of surrounding offices. "They've all spent quality time with Jo-Jo, listening to her views, soaking up the way she talks to people. They are great. If a new subject comes up and they are not sure how she feels about it, they ask her, or they ask me if she's not available. They know what her opinions are on pretty much everything. They do the same for Chuck but he doesn't have so many opinions. He's easier to predict. He's a great guy though, really great. A real all-American boy."

"Lillian seemed to have strong opinions about Chuck."

Roger looked up from the screen and almost made eye contact for a fleeting second. "Sure. Yeah. She does. Chuck is great. We just need to keep an eye on him sometimes, make sure he sticks to the script."

"The script?"

"Okay, who's ready for juice and croissants?" Julia was back and Roger chose to turn his attention to her rather than expanding on the concept of "the script".

"These are the greatest croissants," he said, spraying crumbs as he enthused. "You really need to try them. Feel how warm they are. That smell! It's like being in the bakery just as they come out of the oven. So great!"

He was immediately distracted by something on a screen, leaving me to ponder further why someone with a multi-billion dollar empire would choose to spend so much time building and maintaining a platform for one actress.

7

෨෬

I was inside the cottage, Skyping Caroline, who had just settled down for the evening after putting Maddy to bed. I was trying unsuccessfully to convey to her the extent of the social media control that Roger Rex was exercising over Jo-Jo's reputation, when I heard a tap on the glass of the doors overlooking the pool.

"I have a visitor," I told her. "I'll talk to you later. Love you."

"Hey, man!" Chuck greeted me as I slid the door back. "We thought we'd come over and keep you company." The two children stared up at me from behind the tanned muscles of their father's hairless legs, the crumbs of lunch still clinging on round their mouths. He held up a six pack. "I brought some beers. I thought maybe the kids could use your pool while we talk."

"That would be great," I said, picking up my recorder

and stepping out onto the terrace as the children ran to the water, screaming in happy anticipation.

"How old are they both now?" I asked as I joined him on the loungers, accepting a can of beer and laying the recorder on the paving stone between us, checking that the red light was on before settling back into the cushions.

"Harvey is five, Bette nearly seven. They are two very cool dudes."

"I can see that." I waited a few beats before slipping from casual conversation to interview mode. "So, how did you and Jo-Jo meet?" I asked, although I had read up already on the internet.

"We were in a Californian soap together," he said, his eyes hidden behind aviators as he watched over the children, "when we were both starting out. Well, I was starting out; she had already done some cool stuff, off-Broadway theatre in New York, that kind of thing. She wasn't a star or anything, but she was a proper actress. I just looked right for the part." He shrugged. "I was still a little surfer dude back then, just a kid. If I could have sung a note or played a guitar I probably would have been in a boy band. She was the coolest thing I had ever encountered."

"Cool how?"

"Oh man; she knew so much stuff. She'd read so many books. I mean she had all these degrees from top universities, man, she could talk about anything, explain anything. You know who Tom Wolfe is?"

"Sure. He's dead now."

"Well she knew him. We went to a party at his place. I mean I don't think I had ever even read a book at that stage – apart from comic books obviously. She had numbers in her phone you wouldn't believe; Bowie, Beyoncé, Leonardo, everyone. On the set she could sit around with the director and the writers and they would treat her like she was one of them, asking her opinion about everything. Me, I was happier drinking beers with the crew or going to the beach with a bunch of the other girls from the show. I would never even have plucked up the courage to make a pass at her if she hadn't asked me out on a date."

"She asked you out first?"

"You bet, man. We went to some theatre production together. She'd been given two tickets. I have no idea what it was. I didn't understand a word but I didn't care. She explained everything to me afterwards and suddenly I understood everything. She made me feel smart. I'd always thought I was dumb but she convinced me that I was just uneducated. No one had ever been that nice to me before. I had plenty of girls who fancied me, but never one who wanted to go to the theatre with me and explain stuff as well as getting me into bed. Can you imagine what a turn on that was for a boy just up from the farm?"

"I guess her childhood was very different to yours."

He let out a quick exhalation of breath to indicate just how big an understatement that was. "She'd spent time in Africa as a kid, when Martin was building clinics in refugee camps. She'd lived in New York, spent time in Europe with some older boyfriend who was an orchestra conductor or something. Gianni was his name, I think. He lived in a crumbling old villa somewhere near Florence. Her time with him in Europe was a big influence when it came to creating this place," he gestured vaguely around the buildings. "She could quote Shakespeare or Martin Luther King as easily as *Friends* or *The Simpsons*. I'd never met anyone that educated before in my life. I was always more one for the beach and the basketball court."

"When did you first meet her parents?"

He let out a genuine chuckle. "Not for some time. She kept us pretty separate. I think she guessed that I wasn't exactly the kind of guy they would have picked for her. Once we started getting our picture taken together and got into the magazines she had no choice."

"Martin joked that Lillian was a 'Tiger Mother'."

"That's no joke, man. That woman is fierce, but as a parenting style it sure paid off because she produced a fantastic woman."

"Not your parenting style, I'm guessing."

"Nah. Listen," he grinned like a small boy, gesturing at the two brown bodies wriggling and splashing in the pool, screaming joyfully, "those two already know more than me. They go to this baby school with all these genius kids whose parents run companies in Silicon Valley. All the other dads have IQs of a trillion, and the moms too.

Still beats me what Jo-Jo saw in me. I mean, you should hear the way these people talk ..."

"But I bet your kids are the most beautiful in their classes."

He laughed. "Is that it, do you think? Was that the appeal? Good breeding stock? That's how my dad picks his bulls for the farm."

"Biological urges are a funny old business."

"Hey," he said, lowering his shades to look at me more carefully. "You are a funny dude."

"Maybe she saw that you have a good heart." I shrugged. "So, did you get together immediately after that first date?"

"Pretty much. I could not believe my luck. She was so beautiful. Just looking at her made it hard for me to breathe, let alone talk. She was a couple of years older than me too, and that makes a big difference at that age. I was not the maturest kid on the block, if you know what I mean. I'd had quite a few girlfriends by then, mind you – being a cute-looking surfer boy, you know – and I had a few more afterwards, but once I'd met Jo-Jo none of the others was really going to be able to compete. Know what I mean?"

"Star quality even then?"

"Oh my gosh, yeah. Even on this crappy soap, everyone deferred to her; directors, producers. It was obvious she was going to go on to great things."

"Did you imagine you would end up together?"

"I was never a great one for making life plans, Andy. Apparently I don't have much imagination," he grinned again. "I don't think I thought about it, just enjoyed each day as it came. Looking back now though, I'm pretty amazed. Can't believe my luck. I doubt there's a guy in the whole world who wouldn't occasionally dream of swapping places with me. That's a pretty good feeling."

"What's the idea behind this reality show you're doing?"

"Putting a human face on the superstar. Making her fans feel like they are part of her life, showing us doing normal family type things. It's all Roger's idea. The two of them are thick as thieves. It's great for her to have someone she can talk to about all the smart stuff. I've got nothing to contribute to a discussion on the future of Artificial Intelligence or 'the death of democracy'. Know what I mean? Sometimes I listen to the two of them talking and I only understand about one word in ten. I still hang around though because I just like to hear her talk. Like to watch her lips move. I mean those lips are something else, right?"

"You think this is a 'normal family type thing'?" I gestured at the kids in the pool and the views out across the gardens.

"Yeah," he chuckled. "I know. But the house itself, where we do most of the filming, that's a pretty normal family home. You'll see when you come over. And Jo-Jo's like a normal mom; not running around in black Lycra with a machine gun, taking out baddies like in those films – if you know what I mean. Martin and Lillian make guest appearances now and then too, to give the older folks something to watch. Martin's a bit of a heart-throb with the older women."

"The doctor's bedside manner?"

"He's a great guy. Couldn't ask for a nicer father-in-law. He's never once made me think his daughter is too good for me. Even though she obviously is." He laughed, apparently untroubled by this thought.

"And Lillian has?"

"Like you say, Tiger Mother. No man would ever be good enough for her girl. She's one fully paid up member of the team though."

"The team?"

"Team Jo-Jo. She can say some things you'd rather she didn't, Lillian, but at least you know that she will never lie to you – and a lot of people like to talk shit to you once you get to where Jo-Jo is. They just tell us what they think we want to hear. Lillian will never do that. She sees through all the bull. She is the real deal, know what I mean?"

The kids were screaming at him to join them and he rose to his feet in one easy movement, ran the few steps to the pool and dived in with barely a splash, surfacing beside them with his aviators still perfectly in place, making them shriek with a joyous mock fear as he pretended to be a monster from the deep. It wasn't hard to see what might have attracted Jo-Jo.

8

ഇൻൽൽ

Hi, Andrew, Jo-Jo was texting me. *Everyone's gone out and I am in the house on my own. Want to bring your tape machine and share a bottle of wine?*

On my way, I replied.

I was knocking on the door within three minutes. Jo-Jo was wearing a towelling dressing gown and her wet hair was tied up. She smelled good, fresh from the shower. Sometimes it is hard to concentrate on what you are supposed to be doing, even when all you are doing is listening. She was wearing oversized reading glasses, which made her face look the size of a child's, and carrying a copy of *The Secrets of the Italian Gardener.* One slender finger was acting as a bookmark as she scooped up two glasses and a bottle of wine and gestured for me to follow her to an area of sofas and coffee tables.

Curling up amongst the cushions she poured two glasses of red wine and waved the book at me.

"So is this where it all started, do you think?"

"All what?"

"The groundswell. The change in mood around the world. The dawning of the new age. This is the Arab Spring you're writing about, right?"

"You could call it that. It hasn't turned out that great for most of them."

"The 'Arab Summer' proving a bit elusive?"

"Exactly."

"But do you think that was the moment when ordinary people first realised they could use technology to have a voice of their own in the world? All the stuff that happened in 2016, 2017, 2018; the #metoo thing and #timesup thing, the humiliation of Hillary, the school kids who started speaking up to the NRA about gun control. Did that all start in Tahrir Square?"

"Maybe. Or in Tunisia. But #metoo and so on would probably have happened anyway, sooner or later. There had already been women's suffrage in the West for a century or more, and an end to stuff like child labour. Things were already getting better, at a very slow rate. People were already losing their inhibitions and starting to talk about things that they had been told to be quiet about up till then, to be ashamed of. Abused women and children had been starting to come forward and talk openly about subjects that had previously been considered off limits, no longer afraid of their men or their teachers or their priests or whoever else was abusing them."

"You did a lot of books for people like that, right?"

"A lot, but it took a long time to persuade publishers to take them. Once they discovered how many people wanted to read the stories, however, they couldn't get enough of them. Maybe that was the first stage of the change you're talking about. Maybe technology didn't so much give everyone a voice as magnify the voices that already existed. Do you think? It made people feel they were not alone, that they were part of a larger community. The same with the whistleblowers leaking secret documents from the most tightly locked closets in the worlds of politics or the military. Not so many people dared to do that sort of thing in the past because they would not have felt they could get them out into the public arena fast enough to make a difference and to protect themselves from repercussions."

"Oh, I definitely think so!" She pushed her glasses up into her hair and took a sip of wine, watching me as I pressed "record" and put the tiny machine down on the cushions between us.

"I think this is what it must have felt like at the end of the 1960s and early 1970s for people of my parents' generation," she continued, "when the hippies were rejecting everything that had come before, peace and flowers in their hair, all that great protest music and Jane Fonda telling truth to the establishment about Vietnam and being reviled for it. This is a generational shift like that, I think. A time for big changes."

"All for the good, don't you think?" I checked.

"Sure. Well, there are some downsides, I guess, but on the whole these changes are good. I feel optimistic for my kids' futures."

"Where have the television people gone?" I gestured around the empty room.

"I gave them the afternoon off, so I could spend some time talking to you. And to give Chuck a break."

"Can you remember the first time you set eyes on him?" I asked.

"Chuck? Absolutely, I can," she laughed as she pictured the scene. "It was like seeing the American Dream in human form. He was just so relaxed and carefree. He was on the beach in his shorts and shades, laughing with a bunch of girls. His hair was almost white from the sun that summer and he had that perfect California tan, but it was the smile and the laugh that got me. I heard his laugh before I even heard him speak and I think I fell in love right there and then. He genuinely is as nice and uncomplicated as he seems. Being with him is like breathing pure oxygen. I had had a pretty intense childhood and adolescence and he just seemed to be having so much fun, never troubled by any doubts or guilt about anything. It seemed to me that was an ideal way to be."

"Where is he today?"

"He's taken the kids to the beach at Half Moon Bay."

"He's good with them. He came to visit me at the cottage, brought them for a swim."

"I know. He's a great dad. He's a big kid himself really. Poor Chuck. He never signed up for all of this. He was never happier than when he was in a rubbish soap opera, living the Hasselhoff Hollywood fantasy."

"Isn't this the Hollywood fantasy too?" I gestured round the room where the film crew had left some of their lights and equipment.

"Things aren't as simple any more," she said. "You reach a level where you actually start to have some real leverage in the business and everything changes. When you're a jobbing actor you can live your life pretty much like a kid. Everyone else makes all the decisions on your behalf. They decide what they cast you in, what you are going to wear, how much you should weigh, what you are going to be paid. They decide if you are going to work at all. They tell you where to be and what to do. When they don't need you, you can go to the beach and not think about anything, as long as you have enough money in the bank to pay the bills. Once you've been given a bit of leverage you suddenly have to start making decisions for yourself. You have to take control of situations. You have responsibilities. Most people don't want to be bothered with all that. Most people like having other people make their decisions for them. That's how so many bad guys manage to con their way to power. Most people really don't want that much responsibility so they are happy to hand it over to anyone who offers to take it on, even if those people are bullies and crooks and bullshit salesmen."

"I guess that's one of the nice things about being a ghostwriter. Selling the book is someone else's problem. I can concentrate just on the writing."

"I read you saying on the internet somewhere that Trump got into power because of his ghostwriter."

I laughed, more out of surprise that she had been googling me than anything else. Even though I always googled people I was going to meet or write about I never expected anyone else to bother to do the same to me. It was slightly unnerving, as well as flattering. How much did she know about me? Was it all true or had she read some of the unsubstantiated rumours about books I was supposed to have written but hadn't?

"I was just making a case for how powerful books can be. If Tony Schwartz hadn't written *The Art of the Deal* for him, Trump probably wouldn't have got the Apprentice TV gig; without that exposure he probably wouldn't have won as many votes."

"That's a pretty big responsibility for the ghost."

"It's a pretty big consequence, but I don't think anyone could have foreseen such a bizarre chain of events at the time of writing the book – not even Trump."

"No," she laughed. "It was disappointing when we were so close to getting our first woman president. But maybe Hillary wouldn't have been the best one for such an historic role. Trump did a lot to make the whole process more transparent with his ridiculous tweeting and saying whatever stupid thing came into his fat head. He blew away a lot of the mystique of the ruling class – like pulling back the curtain and revealing the real Wizard of Oz. I've met a lot of men like Trump over the years in Hollywood and in third world dictatorships."

"You're not worried about all the fake news and misinformation circulating everywhere?"

"It was always there, it's just that most people didn't get to see it, or if they did they didn't recognise it for what it was. Those in power, or wanting to get into power, have always operated propaganda machines, paid people to spread the right messages around. That's what we're paying you for, isn't it?" She arched one flawless eyebrow to suggest she was only half teasing. "The news media have always slanted their stories to fit the prejudices of their paying audiences. Even in the 1930s and forties the film studios made up fake back-stories for their stars, pretending they were heterosexual when they weren't, hiding drink problems or worse. Never mind all the lies the leaders tell their people during wars in order to persuade them to risk getting killed. Now the new transparency means we can actually see them doing it and understand a little better how the political and marketing machinery works."

"So, you feel optimistic about things generally?"

"Sure. I think the whole Trump thing was like the death throes of the old white male supremacy crap. It was like a wake-up call to everyone else that it was time to see things differently. John Wayne no longer ruled the world.

In fact people like that had just become embarrassing old men – the sort of pompous old relatives you avoid getting trapped in a corner with at family gatherings. You just have to watch all the old men on Capitol Hill trying to understand how Facebook and Google work. When the old billionaires got back into power, looking for all the world like mafia dons, it galvanised a lot of people into action."

"When Obama came to power – an intelligent, emotionally sound, mixed race guy; I believed it was like an evolutionary step forward, and that it would inevitably lead to a woman in the White House after that, and she might even be mixed race and know something about what the rest of the world is actually like. Maybe she would even be gay! Finding that we had to choose between Hillary and the Donald; that was a wake-up call to tell people like me that we couldn't take liberal progress for granted. There were more reactionary forces out there than we had realised, all keen to drag us back to the Dark Ages, back into the primeval swamp. Most people in the US are immigrants of some sort, so it pretty soon became obvious that Trump and his people were completely out of touch with reality with their ranting against Mexicans and Muslims and everyone else, but there they all were, still in positions of power, holding the purse strings."

"Like mafia dons?"

"Precisely," she gave a giggle and sipped her wine.

"Has being the child of immigrant parents affected you?"

"Of course. Everyone has opinions about Mexican men and about Chinese women. My mother also conforms to a number of the popular stereotypes," she smiled ruefully. "You've met Lillian, right?"

"She made dinner for me my first night."

"Right. Well, there you go."

"So what about the online trolls and death threats and hate speak and all the rest?"

"There were always people with those sorts of views, but in the past we didn't get to hear what they were saying because they only expressed themselves in bar rooms and in private. They had no really effective platforms. We only realised how they truly felt when they had mustered the Dutch courage to go out and lynch or rape someone. Now at least we know what they're thinking and saying before they do that, because it's out there on the Net. We have more 'transparency', as we keep being told. It's unpleasant to read or listen to these people's opinions but better that we understand the extent of their rage so that we can at least try to do something about counteracting it or defusing it. If the democrats had understood better how unpopular Hillary was, what people were actually saying about her behind closed doors, they might have put forward a different candidate, one who would have won in 2016."

I realised I could keep talking like this for ever and I

was wasting valuable time. Someone might interrupt us at any minute, demanding her attention or her presence elsewhere.

"So, what was your childhood home like?"

"We had a lot of different homes because Dad was always travelling to some new ghetto area or third world country to build a clinic. The first place I remember as being our home for any length of time was San Francisco ..."

"What was the house like?"

"Oh, it wasn't a whole house, it was a flat and we had a couple of lodgers too ..."

She was the perfect interviewee as she drank wine and snuggled further and further down into the cushions; fluent, funny, intimate and able to paint word pictures about her early days.

"Tell me about Gianni," I said after a while.

"Gianni?" She seemed surprised. "Wow, you've been doing some research!"

I shrugged, saying nothing, not wanting to tell her my source was Chuck.

"Sure. He was my first serious love interest I guess. An Italian guy. He was a pretty famous conductor. So suave. Much older than me. I met him in London where my mother had sent me to do a music and acting course during a summer vacation. He came to the school to give a master class and that was it. I didn't bother with the rest of the course. He belonged to one of the old aristocratic families in Italy. They owned a great private art collection but they were starting to have to sell things off to pay for repairs to their various properties and tax bills, you know the sort of thing. He took me to some of the sales in places like London and Rome. It was a fantastic education, in every way. That's one of the reasons I enjoyed this," she held up her copy of *The Secrets of the Italian Gardener* again. "Gianni moved in the same sort of circles as your friend."

"How did it end?"

"I'm not sure. He just dropped out of sight. I have a feeling my mother may have had something to do with it. It broke my heart at the time."

"Didn't you want to find him and ask him what happened?"

"I made contact again many years later but at the time I had a lot of other things on my mind," she said, her eyes focusing on a memory she seemed to be dredging up from far away. "And I reasoned that any guy who was willing to be put off by a girl's mother did not deserve to get the girl! You know what I mean?"

"Did you challenge Lillian about it?"

"I kind of did but she just brushed it aside, made me feel stupid for even suspecting she would bother with something so trivial as a summer love affair. I decided to believe her because she is not a woman to take on in a fight unless you have to. I've tried a few times over the years, as has my father, she just never loses." She laughed.

"Some things in life you just have to accept as inevitable, as beyond your power to alter."

After a couple of hours she stopped talking and looked at me intently, as if a sudden realisation had dawned on her.

"You are good at this," she said, prodding my thigh playfully with a dainty bare foot. "I've told you stuff here that I don't believe I have ever told anyone before."

"Good," I said. "When clients say that I know we're going to end up with a good book."

"I feel like I've known you all my life. How do you do that?"

"I have no idea," I laughed, feeling ridiculously pleased with myself, "it must be a knack."

"I think you're being too modest."

"My wife is always telling me that."

I couldn't work out if she was being sincere or just trying to charm me. If it was the latter it was certainly working. She was adorable and I never wanted the session to end.

By the time Chuck got back from the beach with the kids, all of them barefooted and slightly sun burned, we had three hours of tape and nearly a whole bottle of wine had been polished off. Harvey and Bette threw themselves onto the sofa between their mother and me, both talking at once about everything they had seen and done during the day.

"Have you said Hi to Andrew?" Jo-Jo asked.

They both paused, apparently noticing me for the first time. "Hi," they said in unison, suddenly self-conscious.

"Mommy says you live in England," Bette announced. "And that in England you have a queen and princesses ..."

"That's right," I said, "we have all of those things. And some princes too."

"Does the Queen have soldiers to protect her?" Harvey asked, "With guns and missiles and everything?"

"Well, yes," I said, "I guess she does. But her soldiers don't often have to shoot anyone. They keep her pretty safe in other ways."

"John has a gun," Harvey continued. "I've seen it."

Jo-Jo looked momentarily disconcerted. "You've seen John's gun?"

"He hasn't shown me or anything. I saw it under his shirt when he lifted me out of the car at school."

Chuck had now come over to listen too, sipping on a beer, leaving a trail of sand on the terracotta floor.

"He just carries that to keep us all safe when we're travelling around with him," Jo-Jo said. "He won't ever have to use it."

"He might," Harvey said, matter-of-factly, obviously enjoying the fact that all eyes were now on him and that his sister's mouth was hanging open, her eyes wide with potential panic. "If there were some bad guys he would shoot them down!" he shaped his fingers into a mock pistol and pointed it at his sister's forehead.

"Okay, buddy," Chuck scooped him up. "That's enough. Let's get you something to eat."

I felt that they needed some family time and made my excuses, pocketing the tape machine as I went. Walking away from the house towards the silence of the cottage, hearing the children's voices fading behind me and their parents' laughter, I felt melancholy, like I was trapped on the outside of something lovely. I wanted to get back to the cottage so I could Skype Caroline, but I had a feeling that seeing her and hearing her voice would just make me feel even lonelier. Then I remembered it was the middle of the night in England anyway and for a second I felt like I was stranded in a time warp.

9

ℰℭ

On the way back to the cottage I checked my phone, eager for a distraction from the empty feeling of anticlimax I was experiencing, and found a message from Julia, asking me to drop in on Martin because he wanted to talk. I was grateful for the suggestion, not fancying the idea of being on my own after leaving such a cosy, family scene, knowing I wouldn't be ready to escape into sleep for a good few hours and not enjoying the thought of spending that time surfing through the television channels on my own.

"Lillian is working an evening shift at the hospital," he told me as he let me in, "I thought it might be useful for us to spend some time talking about Jo-Jo when she was young. Would it be helpful to look at some old photograph albums?"

"Definitely."

He handed me a pile of albums as he went off to get me

a coffee, since I thought more alcohol would put me in danger of either becoming unduly melancholy or pressing the wrong button on the recorder. The albums had been lovingly put together in a way that families used to do such things, when photographs were still objects with rarity value and not a commodity that you could tap into at will, particularly families who spent a lot of time travelling and needed to keep their memories in order. The pictures, neatly displayed behind mildly adhesive transparent sheets, showed that Jo-Jo had always been stunningly beautiful, both as a small child and as an awkward teen. She even looked good with braces on her teeth and a mild speckling of acne across her cheeks. In many of the African pictures her skin was glistening with sweat and her hair was pulled back so her face could take advantage of any air there might be. She also looked astonishingly comfortable and relaxed whatever country or company she was in, however stark the poverty surrounding her. Many of the pictures showed her cuddled up to people who were obviously deeply sick, probably dying, but she showed no signs of nervousness, no sign that she would rather have been anywhere else. She emanated a joyfulness that made others glow around her. There was no sign of the "intense childhood" she had talked about on the sofa. Whatever stresses she might have been experiencing, she was obviously very skilled at hiding them. Already an actress perhaps.

"You must have been very proud of her," I said when he

returned with the coffee. I turned on my recorder and put it casually on the table beside the cafetière.

"I was. I am. I always knew she was special. Everyone falls in love with her. I expect you will too, if you haven't already. It's the effect she has on people. It's a great gift."

I said nothing as he gave me the coffee and he smiled as if he could see from my face that I had already fallen under her spell.

"She gets cross when I tell her that. She says it's just because I'm her father that I believe it; that I'm biased."

We both laughed because we both knew that wasn't true.

"Her mother used to have the same effect on people. There have been many men who would happily have killed for Lillian in the past."

We sat in silence for a few moments as I turned the pages of the albums, deliberately taking my time, drinking in the places where she had been, imagining what they would have looked like through her eyes at whatever age she might have been, how they would have felt to a young girl, so that I would be able to describe them on the page, as if in her own words.

"They tell me that you can be trusted with all the family secrets," Martin said after a while. "That nothing will get out without Jo-Jo's approval."

"That's right. Roger has some fearsome London lawyers working for him. I've basically signed away my life."

"I think it would be a good idea for me to tell you a

little bit about Lillian's history while she isn't here. Not that I'm talking behind her back. She would tell you herself if you asked, but I think it would be helpful for you to hear a less dramatised version from someone. Or maybe you have already been told some things?"

"Nothing that isn't readily available on the internet; 'daughter of immigrants, working as a midwife', that sort of thing."

"Well, those things are both completely true, but there is more to the story. When I met Lillian I was helping to set up a clinic in Las Vegas."

"Las Vegas? Not your usual beat. Hardly the developing world," I gestured to the albums.

"You'd be surprised. It's possibly got the widest divide of any city in the world between the rich and the poor; did have even then. It is also run by some of the most terrifying people you are ever likely to meet." He laughed. "I had to deal with some pretty gruesome dictators in the developing world over the years, but none of them can match the guys who run Vegas for sheer ruthlessness and greed. The clinic was to help the women who got caught up in the vice machine. It was a sexual health clinic set up mainly for the working girls. Lillian was a patient."

He looked at me closely as if to gauge whether I was shocked by this revelation. I said nothing, glancing down to ensure that the recorder's red light was on.

"She wasn't my patient," he continued after a moment, "there were other doctors there, but she stayed around, volunteering to help with the administration and reception and things like that. She tells me that she did that because she wanted to get to know me; wanted to impress me. If that's true then the plan worked. She was extremely good at bringing order to a dreadfully disorganised operation. She was very bossy even then," he laughed fondly. "It wasn't long before I fell in love with her. She was absolutely beautiful and had some extremely persistent admirers. I helped her to get out of the sex trade and sorted out her training as a midwife, so we could travel and work together."

He paused, sipping his coffee, watching me again. I said nothing, trying to picture this idealistic young doctor trying to help a fallen woman who had obviously set her cap at him.

"I think it is useful for you to know that," he continued after a moment, "because it explains a lot about her character. She was absolutely determined to escape from the poverty that her parents had suffered, and that was the only way she could see to do it. I see a lot of that determination in Jo-Jo, but of course she has always had far more choices than her mother."

"Does Jo-Jo know the whole story?"

"Well, not every detail – what child wants to hear about their parents' sex lives? But she knows what I've just told you. She knew her maternal grandparents well, so she saw that they'd had hard lives, that they were good people, doing their best for their daughter. Personal hardship never meant much to her because she met so many people who were worse off when we were travelling in places like Africa. What riled her, even when she was a little kid, was people being judged and treated unfairly. Still does. How many of her movies have you seen?"

"A lot of them," I admitted, feeling myself blush before I realised he was enquiring into how thoroughly I had researched my subject, not into the sort of escapist movies I spent my money on. "Probably all of them."

"Okay, so you know, a lot of those early ones, the ones based on the video games, they are basically vigilante movies, right? The people she was avenging were nearly always women or poor immigrant workers and the people she went after were always the big white bosses. Right? I mean it's not the most original concept when it comes to entertainment for the masses – I remember watching the original version of *The Magnificent Seven* when I was a teenager; the flawed American heroes saving the poor, helpless little Mexican villagers with their superior fight-ing skills," he made a wry face. "But Jo-Jo made the myth believable, that was why people took to her and wanted her to win, especially when she was killing hundreds of bad guys – the kind of bad guys who most of us hate, if the truth be known. 'Sticking it to the man', I think they would say. I'm pretty sure that a lot of the credibility she brought to those scripts and to the roles was because of the way she felt her mother, and other women like her mother, are mistreated by the world when they are young and in their prime, when they should be having the best times of their lives, not the worst."

He paused for a moment as if trying to calm his own anger at old injustices, and regain his usual level of measured, professional self-control.

"I just thought it would be helpful for you to know that, so you wouldn't be taken by surprise by someone else feeding you inaccurate rumours."

"Transparency is always very helpful," I agreed, aware that I was already starting to sound like Jo-Jo, a good sign when you are hoping to ghost in another's voice. "If I know the truth then I can avoid some of the potential pitfalls."

"There will always be people who will judge someone like Lillian harshly for what she used to do and the sort of people she used to hang out with, but there are more who would judge her harshly if they thought she was lying about her past."

"Absolutely. I think people are very forgiving if they feel they are being told the truth. So, how old would Jo-Jo have been when she found out about her mother's past?"

"I think she learned the truth bit by bit. There were always working girls in the clinics I was setting up, so she would get to know them as people first and then gradually learned what they did for a living. I can't remember exactly when she found out that her mother had lived the same sort of life as those women; I guess she was probably fourteen or fifteen."

"How did she react?"

"With sympathy. It brought them closer. Girls that age can be quite hard on their mothers, especially if their mothers tend to be controlling by nature, but Jo-Jo was always very kind and patient with Lillian."

He paused to top up my coffee.

"I was very pleased when Roger told me you had agreed to do this book. I wasn't sure that you would agree."

"Really?" I was becoming increasingly bewildered by the level of praise I was receiving from all quarters. It had never happened to me on quite this scale before. One of the best things about ghosting is usually the anonymity, which helps the ghostwriter to avoid hearing direct criticism from those who might not like their work. The flipside of that is that you seldom hear any praise either. I was very unsure how to handle it or even if it was sincere. Were they all just being polite? Or were they manipulating me in some way? Either way it was a pleasant experience.

"I told him you would be the best person for the job because I'd read a lot of the books you wrote about subjects like people trafficking, enforced marriages and female circumcision."

"I have you to thank for my being here?"

"Well don't thank me yet. Wait and see how things turn out," he smiled as if to suggest that he knew very well he deserved my gratitude. Or was he actually issuing a friendly warning that things were going to be getting more complicated than I might be expecting?

"I didn't think readers ever noticed the name of the ghost when they bought a book," I said. "On most of them my name doesn't even appear."

"Well it appeared on enough for me to notice. I was considering writing a memoir myself at one time and I thought I might contact you for help with that. I mean, I've published plenty of academic books, but you need very different skills to engage readers at an emotional level. I don't kid myself that I have those skills."

"So you suggested my name to Roger?" I was still having trouble getting my head around how the whole process had happened.

"Absolutely, but I thought you might think that a Hollywood autobiography was too trivial. I told him he should make you an offer you couldn't refuse."

"He did."

"Good," Martin laughed, raising his coffee cup in a mock toast. "He can more than afford it."

"So how did Roger's connection with Jo-Jo start?"

"They are both fascinated by the future and how it can be shaped for the better. Plus they are both techies. They both invest in the same sort of start-ups."

"But he seems to be taking a particular interest in this book."

"You'll have to ask him about that," Martin said and for a moment I thought he was avoiding my eyes.

"How long have you known him?"

"Roger? It must be twenty years now. He makes a point

of talking to people who are working in the voluntary sector. He wants to make plans for how best to use his fortune to benefit mankind. Like Bill and Melinda Gates and Warren Buffett, they all want to find the best way to influence things for the good. Elon Musk thinks that colonising Mars is the best way to help mankind survive. Bill and Melinda think more about fighting infectious diseases and infant mortality. Roger's ambitions lie somewhere between the two extremes. He's passionate about protecting democracy. He was very helpful for fund raising when I needed to put up clinics in areas that most charities tend to avoid."

"So he got to meet Jo-Jo through you?"

"I'm not sure how they first met." He seemed to want to move the conversation on but at the same time obviously didn't want to appear unhelpful. I stayed quiet to see what he would say next. "He used to come to the house a lot to talk when Jo-Jo was still living at home. She would be in the background, listening. I guess that was how she first became interested in the whole technology sector."

"Did they date?" I asked.

He laughed, as if I had given him a way to release some invisible tension. "I'm not sure that Roger has ever done much dating. I don't think he has the time or the brain space for it. I'm not sure he would even know how to ask a girl out. Lillian was forever telling them they would make a great couple. 'With his brains and your beauty ...' she would say. She would have liked nothing better."

"Lillian wanted them to get together?"

"Absolutely. She always had this belief that Roger would be really successful."

"What did Jo-Jo say when Lillian said that?"

"She would just laugh. I don't think she ever thought of Roger as anything more than a friend. She always likes to please her mother, but there are limits, aren't there?"

He fell silent as if casting his mind back to very different times. I said nothing, waiting for something to emerge, not wanting to interrupt the flow of his memories.

"They were exciting times around here, with all the technology companies taking off at the same time," he said. "It felt like the whole world was changing and we were right at the centre of the perfect storm, watching them inventing the future. I was very optimistic in those days, believing that we were actually going to find ways to make the world a fairer, better place. I thought technology was going to eradicate poverty, improve health; everyone was going to get clean water and no one would have to go hungry. Utopia, I thought, was just around the corner."

"You don't feel that any more?"

"It can definitely be done, but it is taking much longer than I thought then. I hadn't realised how reluctant most people were to embrace change and how slowly the improvements would come. I didn't foresee how ludicrously rich and powerful the successful tech companies would become; how they would exacerbate the gap between rich and poor, creating a whole new strata of super-rich above everyone else, a group of people who would become totally divorced from the real world."

"People like Roger."

"Indeed, but he is one of the better ones. I actually believed that we would have seen an end to war and an end to hunger by now ..."

"And Jo-Jo was listening and learning all this?"

"Absolutely. At the time I didn't realise quite how deeply she was thinking about everything. A lot of her time was spent on getting her acting career going; it was only later, once she started getting a platform and speaking out that I realised just how deeply she felt about social issues. Roger had a lot of input into how her mind was developing during those years."

"So, why is he taking so much interest in this book – and in Jo-Jo's 'platform'?" I asked again.

"He believes she can make a difference," he shrugged. I waited to see if he would add anything else. "She is also very popular with a huge section of the public. Guys like Roger are not as popular as they used to be. When they were all young geeks inventing things in their garages or in their university dormitories it was all very exciting and romantic and appealing. Everyone was rooting for them to get rich and live the dream. Everyone fantasised about doing the same thing, inventing something world-changing that would make them rich beyond their wildest dreams. Once they became middle-aged men and hired armies of lawyers to help them get out of paying their fair share of the taxes, they became less attractive. Those early revolutionaries have now become the establishment figures that other people dream of over-throwing. Roger is well aware of this change in public perceptions. Through Jo-Jo he has a way of talking to people who wouldn't want to listen to a middle-aged, white, male billionaire."

I kept silent for a little longer but he had said all he intended to say at that stage.

"That," he said eventually, "is what we mean when we talk about Jo-Jo's 'platform'."

10

☯

"The kids have got something for you," Chuck said as I came into the house. The film crew were busy with Jo-Jo and Lillian as they made a meal together at the other end of the room and we were able to stay out of camera shot on the sofas.

"I drew this," Bette announced. "It's a princess from England."

"That is fantastic," I said, taking the picture. "What is her name?"

"Princess Bette."

"You're not a princess," her brother announced, handing me his picture. Bette ignored him, snuggling close in order to give Harvey's artwork her full critical attention. It seemed they were now comfortable in my company, which felt like a major personal victory.

"My brother likes soldiers," she told me. "He's always shooting me."

"I hope not," I said. "He should be protecting you, not shooting you, especially if he's a soldier and you are a princess."

"Some of the red is blood," Harvey told me as I studied the scene he had created, "but some of it is the soldiers' coats. Dad found me a picture of the Queen's guards and they wear red coats and weird furry hats which cover their eyes."

"How do they shoot if they can't see?" Bette asked. "How do they even march anywhere?"

"They can sort of peer out underneath to see where they are going," I said. "But I think they take the hats off if they want to actually fight. They're called bearskins."

"The hats are made of bears' skins?" Harvey asked.

"I believe they are," I said, regretting stepping into the territory I was now entering.

"So the soldiers shoot the bears to get their skins?"

"They take the bears' skins to make hats?" Bette's eyes were once again wide with horror. "That is so mean."

"I'd like to go bear hunting," Harvey said, miming how he would fire his imaginary hunting rifle, picking off each member of the television crew as they circled silently around his mother and grandmother at the other end of the room.

Lillian and Jo-Jo were arguing as they cooked and seemed to have forgotten that the cameras were there, although that may have been more to do with their acting skills. Lillian was stir-frying noodles and Jo-Jo had a cake in the oven, a few white dabs of flour on her cheeks emphasising the perfect olive tones of her complexion.

"Confucius never believed in democracy," Lillian was saying. "He didn't think ordinary people should be the ones to elect political leaders. He thought the people were too stupid to make decisions for themselves. Not everyone is created equal, not everyone has a right to self-government."

"Maybe we should go more with the ancient Greeks then, Mama?" Jo-Jo suggested, pulling the cake out and testing it with a skewer.

"The Greeks? Pah! You think they know what they're doing? They are going down the plug hole! We can chuck out all this food if you want and make moussaka. You would do that to your children? You would make them starve like the children of Greece?"

I could see that Jo-Jo was laughing now, but Lillian was not, taking her anger out by prodding the stir fry hard as it sizzled on the top of the oven. I could see why so many people were enjoying the show; I hadn't seen many reality shows where the participants were likely to be found comparing Greek and Confucian philosophies in the kitchen. The film crew were shooting us dirty looks for making too much background noise.

"Can we go swimming in Andy's pool?" Harvey asked his father.

"What's wrong with your pool here?"

"It's boring."

"You'll have to ask Andy. He might have had enough of us."

They both turned to look at me, pleading with their mother's eyes.

"Sure," I said. "Why not? If you're not needed for filming."

"Filming is boring," Bette said.

"She's not wrong," Chuck said and the four of us left for the cottage.

* * *

This time I went into the pool with them and Chuck devised a succession of games for us all. He was tireless when playing with them and never seemed to grow bored. Throwing the children back and forth between us, listening to their joyful screams and splutterings as they went under the water, made me feel homesick. It should have been Maddy I was chucking up in the air and catching, not someone else's children, no matter how charming they might be. It reminded me of times I had spent in the local public pool with Becky, when she was small, and that made me feel sick to think how much I had lost the day she died and guilty about the pleasures I was deriving from a glittering Californian pool and someone else's children.

After a couple of hours Jo-Jo joined us, having been released by the film crew, and I was able to leave the tape machine running as the conversation ambled back and forth.

"You and Lillian have very different political views," I said, "judging from the conversation in the kitchen."

"Yeah," she laughed, "I guess. Political views come out of your experiences, don't they? It's easy to be a liberal and a democrat when you have always been secure and loved and never in any real danger of starving. My views might be more like hers if my childhood had been more like hers."

"Did you argue about politics when you were growing up?"

"Not much. It's pretty hard to win an argument with her and it's impossible to change her views. I have seen a lot of people try over the years, particularly when we were living in the developing world amongst do-gooders and charity workers. I never saw anyone succeed."

"Tell me more about the countries you remember most vividly from your childhood."

Every so often I would interject a specific question in order to trigger her memory and to get her to describe some event or person from the past. I was aware that by allowing her to ramble I was giving myself a lot of recordings to go through once I was home, but I didn't think it would be a great hardship to have to relive such an idyllic afternoon once back in my office, staring out the window at grey British skies. As the heat of the afternoon sun relented, we all walked to Lillian and Martin's house so that the kids could eat before they went home to bed.

"You need to come and visit me," Lillian told me as we

were leaving. "I can tell you so many things you need to know."

"That would be great," I replied. There was something about the intensity of her manner which still unnerved me; even now I was getting to understand her back story.

It took me a long time to get to sleep that night and then I forgot to put my phone on silent, which you should always do if you are in a different time zone and people back home don't know, so it woke me at four, just after I had dozed off. I could see the caller was a publisher from one of the big conglomerates in London. I should have killed the call and silenced the phone but when you've been a self-employed writer as long as I have you never like to miss a call from a publisher. I had spent too many years begging for their attention to risk ignoring them now I had it.

"Hi, Giles," I tried to sound wide awake.

"Hi, you sound terrible. Have I woken you up?"

"It's okay."

"I have. Where are you?"

"California."

"I'm so sorry. I'll hang up and call you later, once I've checked the time difference."

"No, it's okay. I wasn't really sleeping properly – jet lag, you know."

"Okay, if you're sure. So, you're in California?"

"Yes."

"So the rumours are true?"

My stomach lurched and toppled over what felt like a precipice.

"What rumours?"

I really have to concentrate when I'm preparing myself to lie because I am so bad at it, and the fact that I am concentrating makes me sound even less convincing. Being half asleep was also not helping.

"I heard you were writing for a certain film star."

"No," I tried to laugh casually. My stomach was still falling, visions of lawyers and contracts and court rooms swimming through my head. "I'm on holiday."

"Without Caroline?"

"Yeah, well it's a bit of work too. Combining the two, you know. Caroline couldn't make it. She's got a book coming out." I tried to deflect the conversation.

"I know, I heard." He fell silent, probably waiting for me to blurt something indiscreet. Had Caroline let something slip to one of her friends in publishing? It didn't seem likely. She was the most discreet person I had ever met.

"How are things with you?" I asked, desperately trying to change the subject.

"Listen," he said, "I won't keep you, since it's the middle of the night for you. I just want to make sure that you are thinking of us. We would really want to be considered for this book – unless there is already a publisher on board?"

"Really, Giles," I choked, "I'm just on holiday."

"Okay, whatever you say, but please don't forget us. It

would almost certainly be a high seven figure deal. I'm going now. Go back to sleep."

He hung up and I silenced the phone. The thumping of my heart was making me feel nauseous. How could this possibly have got out? Had I accidentally said something careless to someone? Even though I was sure I hadn't, the lawyers were going to think I had. They would destroy me. There was now no chance I would be going back to sleep any time soon.

11

ಇಂಬ

"Hi, Andy, how's everything going?" Julia always opened her calls in the same tone, like she had nothing better to do with her day than chat with me, and then ended them the moment she had imparted whatever news or instructions she wanted to impart.

"Fine thanks." A renewed wave of sickness flooded over me. Had Roger already found out that someone had leaked? Was I about to be sacked or sued, made to hand back the first payment?

"Roger wanted to check if you are getting all the access that you need to Jo-Jo."

"Well I could do with a few more sessions, but she is being pretty generous with her time, considering how much of it the television people take up."

"Okay, we'll see if we can schedule in some more one-on-one meetings for you. In the meantime Lillian asked if you would like to go over to see her. She's off work today and Martin is away at Stanford at a conference. She's found some more memorabilia from Jo-Jo's childhood."

"That would be great. I'll go over now." I was on the verge of mentioning the call I had received in the night but lost my nerve and hung up.

Lillian was playing with an iPad when I arrived.

"Have you been avoiding me, Mr Ghostwriter?" she asked in a tone which I suspect she thought was flirtatious but was actually slightly intimidating.

"No, of course not," I laughed nervously, "Roger and Julia have been keeping me pretty busy. And I've been getting to know your grandchildren."

"They don't trust me."

"Who?"

"Roger and his people."

"What do you mean?"

"Roger talks all the time about the importance of trust. He says if people don't trust the internet it will never fulfil its potential. He blames the media and the politicians. He says if we don't trust our politicians we will never get trustworthy ones. He says that all the time, but he doesn't trust me."

I tried to read from her expression whether she was joking but she was still staring at the iPad. She waved for me to sit down.

"There," she said eventually, handing it to me, "there are all the essays that Jo-Jo wrote at school."

"You photographed them?"

"Sure. Paper can get lost or stolen. They will give you an important insight into how clever she was as a little girl. I was clever too, but my parents couldn't afford to give me a good education. Don't read them now. You can take the iPad with you. She had so many good ideas when she was little. She wanted to save the whole world."

Lillian laughed at the memories and I waited for her to go on.

"She had time to think because she didn't have to go out to work every evening and weekend. I had to work from a very young age, doing jobs I would never want her to do. You want me to tell you about how I met Martin?"

I switched on the recorder as she sat down beside me and described what life was like as an escort in Las Vegas, and how Martin had seemed to her like a saint, a guardian angel sent by the gods to rescue her and to give her life a purpose.

"He was so good looking," she purred. "He is still good looking, of course, but now he is an old man. Then he was like a film star. He and Jo-Jo are very close. Jo-Jo loves her daddy so much."

When I took out my phone on the way back to the cottage a couple of hours later, I saw that I had a number of missed calls and messages, all of them from blue chip publishers asking me to get back to them. There were emails too, including one from Caroline.

Everyone wants to know where you are and what you are doing. I think someone might have leaked about who you are working for. Have told them all to go fuck themselves. Beware of the lawyers. Assure them nothing has leaked from this end – unless you've been shooting your mouth off in some sleazy bar somewhere, of course – ☺ xxx.

It was a relief to know that she hadn't accidentally told anyone because I was certain, now that I had thought about it calmly, that I hadn't. Over the previous few hours I had sort of decided to ignore the publisher's call in the night and just hope that no one else mentioned it. This deluge was different. There was no hiding the fact that someone had let slip what I was here for. I was going to have to let Roger know what was happening. I rang Julia.

"You need to warn Roger," I said, "someone seems to have leaked to the publishing world that I am here. I am getting lots of calls."

"Okay, Andy, thank you for letting me know, I will get right back to you."

She rang back five minutes later, just as I was settling down to read Jo-Jo's essays.

"Roger says are you free to meet this evening?"

"Sure."

"Okay. I'll come pick you up about six."

For the next few hours I read all the essays that Lillian had committed to the computer. She was right; they showed an extraordinary understanding of the ways of the world and equally extraordinary depths of compassion, mixed with practical suggestions for how to improve things. She was writing about the genocides in Bosnia and Rwanda, and the end of apartheid in South Africa as eloquently and knowledgeably as she talked about the possibilities of the World Wide Web. There was a piece about the trial of O. J. Simpson, which went into the effects of fame and hero-worship on the psyche, another about the Waco bombing in Texas and another about Schindler's List and the Oscars ceremony. I became so engrossed in the material, so able to picture the earnest young girl who had penned them, that I was taken by surprise when Julia rang a few hours later to say she was outside in the Tesla.

12

❧

"Can you explain the publishing industry to me?" Roger said the moment I walked through the front door and the Tesla had purred away down the mountain. The house was a series of vast open spaces like the office, more glass and pale wood stretching forever between scattered art works of daunting size and modernity, and clumps of chairs and couches. "I don't get it."

"It's the most inefficient business model imaginable," I said, sinking into a low, Scandinavian looking chair opposite him, certain now that I was about to be fired. "And very small scale compared to anything happening around here. Most books only sell a few hundred units. Mostly it's like a cottage industry with a few gigantic hits disguising that fact – the Harry Potters and the James Bonds, the Fifty Shades of Grey, they are what keep the publishers afloat."

"Seriously? A few hundred units?"

"Seriously. Some even less. You only have to sell a few thousand copies in one week to get into the bestsellers charts."

"That's amazing. Do you think we should offer this project to the big publishers?"

It was time to face the music. "I think someone has already been talking to them," I said. "I've been receiving calls from almost all of them."

"Yeah, that was me," he said. "I talked to a woman I know. Does news really travel that fast in the analogue world?"

"Of course it does." I felt a wave of relief. "I thought this was supposed to be a secret project. The lawyers had me signing a thousand bits of paper, promising to kill myself before revealing that it existed or that I had anything to do with it."

"You know what lawyers are like," he swatted the whole idea of confidentiality away like an irritating insect. "I just wanted to get a feel for the market and who would be interested, so I rang a woman I was at school with who knows about these things. I told her you were involved to show that it was a serious prospect, to show them it will actually happen. I imagine they get ideas for books pitched to them all the time, right?"

"Absolutely."

"I wanted to catch their interest."

"Well, they are all interested." I held my phone up to show him the list of missed calls.

"So, would there be any advantage for us to go with one of the big ones?"

"In most cases I would say wait to see how much they are offering as an advance, but I'm guessing money isn't really the issue here."

"Not if we're only likely to sell a few hundred copies," he snorted.

"That was an average book I was talking about, not a film star's autobiography. You might sell a million or more on Jo-Jo's reputation."

"And what percentage does an author get?"

"It would probably average out at about fifteen per cent of the cover price, given how much they are likely to want the book, maybe twenty if you send those scary lawyers in to negotiate."

"You're kidding me." He seemed genuinely shocked, actually looking directly into my eyes for several seconds as if certain that I must be teasing and determined to laser the truth out of me.

"Afraid not. You would also lose virtually all control over the book. The publisher would decide when to publish and how to package it. If you self-publish with a small independent you get to keep total control and keep virtually all the money apart from the expenses of hiring an editor, cover designer, printer and so forth. That way the author probably ends up keeping eighty per cent of whatever money the book earns."

"So, who would do all the work on making the physical book happen?"

"There are a lot of independent publishers in the market doing all the same things as the big publishers; freelance editors, designers, all the rest. My wife does that sort of thing."

"But the big guys would be better at marketing, right?"

"Not necessarily. Everyone in publishing is grossly underpaid and over-worked – apart from a few people right at the top. The chances are that someone in your marketing department would have far more time and expertise than any publisher's PR person – or maybe someone in Jo-Jo's own entourage, or from the production company that's doing the reality show for you."

"So, we should self-publish, you think?" He was staring at me intently again, as if trying to read my brain. Given how hard he usually found it to even make eye contact for a second, I could imagine how intimidating his stare would be in a business negotiation.

"Unless one of the big publishers offers an advance which is so huge it changes the whole game, I would say yes."

"Okay. I think you're right but why don't you talk to a few of these guys who are contacting you? Get a feel for what they might be able to offer, pick their brains a bit and then we'll decide."

A Filipino houseboy appeared at the far end of the room carrying a tray of health drinks and burgers. We watched in silence as he approached; his footsteps the only sound.

"You want to eat? You can interview me about Jo-Jo at the same time." Roger asked, waving for the boy to carry the food onto the terrace so we could sit outside and listen to the night insects while Roger explained to me how he and Jo-Jo had first met and started investing together.

I remained quiet, letting my recorder soak up the information, occasionally interjecting a question in an attempt to ascertain just how much money the two of them must have made together. The figures, however, were beginning to grow so large I was having trouble even envisaging what they would look like if written on the page. The actual money didn't seem to be of any interest to him, just the ideas and the products and the changes in people's lives that resulted. He didn't see the accrual of wealth as an achievement, just as a necessary step to fund his research and the development of products that would change the world for the better.

"We have so many opportunities opening up to really make a difference," he said, "to really improve life for everyone. We have to find ways to speed things up."

13

෨ා෨

"Wanna come pick the kids up from school with me?" Chuck asked, finding me at a loose end on his kitchen sofa while Jo-Jo was being filmed doing yoga exercises with a group of other young actors and actresses in her exercise studio.

"Sure."

We walked out to the courtyard, unnoticed by any of the film crew, towards the mighty Mercedes six-wheeler that Chuck told me was Harvey's favourite car.

"What is it exactly?" I asked.

"Mercedes G63 AMG," he told me, the grin of a true enthusiast lighting up his face. "It was originally designed by the Australian Army, so it's great in the desert. Sheikh Mohammed drives one in Dubai. Harvey thinks we should mount guns on the bonnet."

Climbing up into the leather seats it was not hard to

understand why it would appeal to a small boy who was currently obsessed by soldiery in all its forms.

"Doesn't it make you a bit conspicuous?" I asked as we set off towards the gates.

"Yeah a little bit. Jo-Jo really wants me to get rid of it because it's so bad for the environment. All the geek dads like to drive Teslas and Toyotas. I told her she has to convince her son first. So far she hasn't had any luck. Thank God!" he laughed, pressing his bare foot to the floor. "I guess in a few years' time he'll go all new-agey like the rest of his school friends."

"What will you do then?"

"Buy a racing bike I guess. Save the planet and get fit at the same time."

I could see what he meant when we got to the school gates. There were lines of expensive cars, all of them discreet and anonymous looking. A lot of heads turned as he parked the monster luxury truck and hopped out to join the other waiting parents. Most of them, I noticed, were women, or men who looked like John.

"Not many fathers on the school run," I commented.

"Not many mothers either," Chuck laughed. "Most of these guys are nannies or au pairs or housekeepers or something. All the guys with shades and ear pieces are security. Everyone is paranoid about kidnapping attempts."

"Aren't you?"

He shrugged. "Can't live your life in fear, man."

As the doors of the school opened and the children rushed out towards us there was a sudden burst of joyous noise. They were all shouting and laughing at the tops of their voices, the teachers trying to be heard above them.

It was only when I saw the blood that I realised the screams were not joyous any more and the popping noises that had preceded them were gunshots. All the men that Chuck had pointed out to me as bodyguards woke up to what was happening at the same moment as me and jumped into action, pulling guns from inside their jackets or from under their shirts, shouting orders at the nannies and children as they scanned the crowd, searching for the source of the bullets at the same time as seeking out their particular charges from the chaos of running and falling bodies. Their trained voices shouted military orders at kids who couldn't hear beyond their own screams and those of their friends.

My first instinct was to fall to the ground, but what if the bullets were coming from above and I was making myself into a stationery target? Next instinct was to run for cover, but if I couldn't work out which direction the bullets were coming from I couldn't work out which walls would offer cover, or which direction offered escape. No more than five seconds can have passed before I realised I couldn't run because I had to help get the children to safety. But which children? It should probably be Harvey and Bette before anyone else, but where were they? Should

I help the child nearest to me, a small girl who had sunk to the ground clutching her head, blood bubbling up between her fingers? What should I do with her? Should I carry her away from the scene? Which direction was the safest? I was frozen to the spot, anchored by indecision.

No more than ten seconds had passed when I heard one of the bodyguards shout that he had spotted the killer on the roof and the other professionals fanned out to surround the building, all staying low, guns cocked, muttering into microphones. The shots kept raining down. How long would this go on before someone shot him or he decided he had finished his job and made a run for it?

When I turned back I saw that Chuck was also running, crouched low, into the midst of the scattering children, searching for Harvey and Bette. Even bent double he made a conspicuous target, his bright blond hair and pink beach shirt clearly visible both to his children, as they ran towards him, and to the gunman, watching from above. As Chuck leaped on top of the kids, crushing them under the weight of his body, the bullets struck his head, spraying all three of them in his blood. If Harvey and Bette were screaming, the sound was muffled by their father's dead body. I suspect they had had the breath knocked out of them and were unable to make any sound. I got down on all fours and crawled as fast as I could manage towards them. Everything seemed to move hideously slowly, like I was struggling to force my limbs forward through a sea of treacle.

The private bodyguards had now been joined by the school's own security guards who had appeared on the roof from inside the building, and between them they managed to pin the shooter down into a corner. There was a roar of return fire and then silence as they hit their mark. In the following few seconds most of the screaming turned to moaning and sobbing.

Reaching Chuck's body after what seemed like an eternity I rolled him off the blood-splattered children. I lifted one child up under each arm and ran back towards the Mercedes. My first thought was to get them away from the scene. Maybe I thought that the less time they had looking at the mess their father's face had become, the less well they would be able to remember the sight later. It was not a logical decision. I'm not sure it was even sensible, but it was the one which came to me and made my legs move faster than they ever had before.

There was so much of Chuck's blood on them it was hard to tell if they had been hit themselves, but they seemed to be breathing okay, just shaking and crying. Opening the back door I threw both of them onto the seats and climbed in with them, slamming the door after us, shutting out the noise and chaos. Both of them were now crying quietly, all of us white faced and trembling as I tried to steady my hand enough to dial Julia.

"There's been a shooting at the kids' school," I said as soon as she answered, trying in vain to keep my voice steady. "Chuck's been hit. Tell Jo-Jo and send someone to come and get us."

"Where are you?" she asked.

"Parked outside the gates in Chuck's truck. I think they've got the shooter, but we need to get the kids out of here and I don't have a key to drive this thing." There was no way I was going to let Harvey and Bette see me rummaging through their fallen father's pockets for an ignition key and I was certain I wasn't in a fit state to drive anyway.

The Tesla arrived a few minutes after the police and ambulances. There was so much chaos that John was able to transfer the kids between vehicles without anyone noticing. Both children were crying more loudly now, wanting their mother and asking where Chuck was and why he wasn't coming with us.

"John will get you back to Mummy," I assured them, "I'll go find Daddy. The doctors will be helping him now."

"Is he dead?" Harvey asked, fascinated despite his terror at being thrown into the front line of a real-life battle.

"I think he just fell over and bumped his head," I lied. "I'll go find him."

"We need to go," John told me.

"You take them," I said. "I need to talk to the police. I can't just disappear from the scene."

"I'll come back for you."

He sped away and I made my way into the throng, searching for Chuck. There were a lot of wounded people shivering under blankets and being tended to by emergency workers and well-wishers. I recognised his bare feet sticking out from under a blanket that someone had used to cover his head and body. It wasn't the only covered body, but it was the biggest. Taking a deep breath I tweaked the blood-soaked corner of the blanket back. His eyes were still open. I retched but wasn't actually sick.

"Do you know him, Sir?" a voice asked and I found a police woman standing above me.

"Yes," I replied. "He's Jo-Jo Win's husband, Chuck."

"Second name?"

"Huck, Charlie Huck."

"He's an actor too, right?"

"Yeah."

"What's your relationship to the deceased, Sir?"

"Family friend. I came with him to pick up the kids from school."

"Where are the kids now?"

"They've gone back to their mother. I wanted to get them away from this."

"I'm going to need to take some details, Sir."

14

ഇൻൽ

By the time I had got back to the cottage, texted Caroline a wobbly two-word message, "Am okay", and logged on to the internet, the shooting had become the top news item across the western world. The killer, who was apparently now confirmed as having been shot dead, had posted a video on YouTube a few hours earlier, explaining what he was planning. It seemed that he was a disillusioned worker from Google. He had a litany of personal complaints against the company itself and then started to ramble about how the big tech companies were taking over the world, sucking all the wealth out of the system, created monopolies and avoided paying taxes, thereby increasing levels of poverty for the rest of American society. It was a familiar complaint but an unusually draconian response to set out to slaughter the children of as many billionaires and multi-millionaires as possible. If his goal had been to focus world attention on the wealth gap, he had certainly succeeded, but he had also succeeded in making some sections of the population actually feel sorry for the "one per cent", giving them a vulnerable, human face, if only temporarily. Pretty much everyone agreed that no matter how many billions of dollars you had, nothing could compensate for having a child murdered.

There was a glazed look in the man's eyes as he delivered his message, which some commentators took to indicate insanity while others said it was undoubtedly the result of a large intake of drugs. Some people latched on to a suggestion that he had actually been hypnotised and manipulated by someone else and was as much a victim as the children whose short lives had been ended, sprawled on the tarmac. A few were already coming up with half-baked suggestions as to who might be behind such an atrocity. Islamic fundamentalists were the most obvious suspects, although there was no indication that the killer had any interest in any religion, either Islamic or Christian, and no terrorist group had claimed responsibility. The government was the next easy target for accusations. One thread suggested that the President was sending out a mob-like warning to the billionaires who were avoiding paying their taxes.

The killer's actual message was not an original or complex economic argument, which was lucky because I was having difficulty decoding any of this barrage of information. I was also having trouble stopping myself from shaking physically as the immediate adrenaline rush of the previous few hours began to wear off, leaving me drained and frightened.

Even more shocking than the crime itself, in a way, was the fact that some internet trolls were already coming out in support of the killer's actions, responding contemptuously to those who voiced any sympathy for the victims. It was as if he had unleashed a torrent of pent-up frustration and hate from those parts of society who had believed as children that geeks were there to be mocked and bullied and who could not now accept that such stereotypically inferior physical specimens had become the rulers of the modern world. Ten minutes spent reading these messages and I began to imagine an army of angry citizens marching on the gates of the estate with pitchforks, intent on lynching all those found cowering inside.

Although the initial headlines in the traditional media outlets were all about the slaying of innocent children, there were already rumours bobbing to the surface online that Chuck was also one of the victims. Just as prominent, however, were rumours that these same reports of Chuck being a victim were "fake news". A surprisingly large number of people seemed to be desperate to verify whether it was true or not. I could understand it being a matter of urgency for anyone who knew him or was related to him, but there was far too much activity for it to be just that. Everyone seemed to want to know everything "now" and sprayed out blame in all directions at what they saw as a deliberate attempt by some unnamed "authorities" to keep the truth from them for as long as possible.

* * *

Not for the first time it occurred to me what a vulnerable place celebrity can be. A woman like Jo-Jo could never hope to melt into the crowd and escape into anonymity if the mood of the people turned against her. Wherever she went someone would recognise her and once she was recognised the crowd around her would know everything about her, while she knew nothing about them as individuals, apart from the fact that they might hate her and see her as an enemy and as a part of whatever problems they might be facing in their lives. I snapped off the computer and went to lie beside the pool with a drink to try to calm down. When my hands were steady enough to be more coherent, I texted Caroline again to assure her I was okay. I didn't feel ready to Skype her, certain that if I saw her face and tried to speak I would break down.

Unable to resist I went back to the internet half an hour later and noticed that there was already a change of mood. The identities of the victims were beginning to emerge. Most were children but there were a few adults, mainly nannies. The pictures were nearly all of young and pretty faces and even the sympathies of the haters were definitely moving in their favour, apparently forgetting that they were the families and employees of the rich. I guess it is hard for all but the most bitter of class warriors to see a small child or a nanny as an enemy worthy of execution when confronted with a picture.

Images of Chuck were also starting to proliferate, many of them from his childhood and his early days as an actor and pin-up, and the storyline emerging was of a simple, all-American boy being destroyed by his own good fortune. There were pictures of him working down on the farm with his father, looking for all the world like Huckleberry Finn. His golden teenage years, which had been captured for posterity by the soap opera cameras and thousands of production publicity stills, depicted the carefree years of a youthful, prosperous America, tapping into a nostalgia for something that had probably never really existed for most of the population. There were shots and clips of him on the beach, kissing girls, laughing with friends, doing push ups to demonstrate the youth, vigour and beauty of his physique. All of it had obviously been scripted and staged by the publicity people of the time, but it fitted with the image of the sociable, barefooted boy-man who had just given his life trying to protect his golden-haired kids from a mad, embittered, lone gunman.

Chuck was being transformed into a national hero before my eyes and, as part of the story, the face of the brave, tragic, beautiful widow was also starting to trend – the predominant storyline here was of a woman who was known, deep in the film-going psyche of the nation, as a righteous but deadly vigilante. She had now been truly and terribly wronged in real life. So what, everyone was subconsciously wondering, would she do about it? Although still in a state of shock, my writing instincts were starting to craft the events into a useable narrative as I tried to make sense of what had happened, tried to divine a meaning that would provide an arc for the story I had been hearing and thinking about ever since I had touched down at San Francisco Airport.

Were any of these rumours Roger's work? Were he and his army of screen-dwellers working flat out in their primary coloured, cushioned lair, pushing back the wave of negative stories, washing them away with an unstoppable tide of positive ones? Were they actually able to turn public perceptions around this quickly? If so, it was an awesome superpower for any one man to possess.

I tuned into a news bulletin on the television just in time to see Chuck's face, amongst several others. They were all being named as casualties of the attack and their total was increasing even as I watched. It had reached twenty by the time I switched off the sound and answered a Skype call from Caroline on my tablet, hoping I was going to be able to hold my emotions in check. She looked like she had only just got out of bed.

"Are you okay? The shooting is on the news over here."

"Yes, I'm okay," I said, feeling the tears coming, "I was

there with Chuck. We were picking up the kids. He's been shot." The words were making me choke.

"Are you on your own? You shouldn't be on your own."

"No, I guess not."

"You'll be in shock."

"I know." My phone rang and I saw Julia's name. "Hang on a sec, I'll just answer that."

"I'm coming to move you," Julia said. "Pack your stuff and wait there."

"Move me where?" I asked, but she had already gone.

"They're moving me somewhere," I told Caroline.

"I heard. Moving you where? Why do you need to be moved? Shouldn't you be telling the police what you saw?"

"I gave them my details at the scene. I guess they'll be following up. I'm not exactly hard to find as long as I am with these people. I have to pack. I'll get back to you when I know what's going on."

"Be careful."

"I will." The moment I hung up I regretted that I hadn't told her how much I loved her. I thought about ringing back but decided against it. I would text her as soon as I was packed and ready to move.

15

J ulia was tapping on the glass at the cottage a few minutes later and I could hear the sound of helicopter rotors in the background as I slid back the doors.

"There are packs of media at all the gates," she said, grabbing one of my cases to hurry me out through the gardens. "We are going to have to fly you out."

A roar of wind ripped through the trees and flattened the foliage either side of the path as a helicopter lifted off from behind the house and flew low across the grounds.

"Jo-Jo and the kids are on that one," Julia shouted. "You are going with Lillian and Martin in the next one. I'll bring the cases in the car."

"Where are we going?"

The roar intensified as the second engine started up and I couldn't hear her answer. She pointed to a lawn where I could see Lillian and Martin running, bent double beneath the whirling blades. She gave me a quick wave and disappeared around the corner with my cases. By the time I reached the door the others were already squeezed into the back and I climbed in next to the pilot, buckling myself in as instructed.

* * *

Five seconds later we were in the air, skimming low across the palm trees and terracotta roofs, getting a bird's eye view of the elegant geometry of the estate. As we lifted up over the perimeter wall I saw the Tesla nosing its way out of the main gates through the crowd of photographers and camera crews. It was astonishing how quickly they had managed to get there. A flicker of movement in the sky caught my attention and I realised we were not the only helicopter above the estate. The big television networks were getting their aerial shots, watched by a hovering police surveillance team. No doubt pictures of our escape were already being beamed out to the world's screens, like the live pictures of O J Simpson's white Bronco being chased down the Los Angeles Freeway prior to his arrest, accused of murdering his wife and her lover; except that none of us was being accused of doing anything wrong. Everyone was watching everyone, none of us knowing what was going to happen next. Most days we take for granted that our lives will follow a relatively predictable pattern. Occasionally those patterns are disrupted by sudden, unforeseen events, which happen too quickly for us to even have time to grow anxious. Very seldom do you look into your future with no idea of what is going to happen next. It is not a comfortable feeling, exciting but not comfortable.

One of the television helicopters followed us for a while as we circled round the hills. Our pilot was talking to someone else, who I guessed was the pilot carrying Jo-Jo and the kids. The plan seemed to be to confuse the press that wouldn't know which chopper she was in and would give up bothering to chase both of us. We criss-crossed back and forth a few times and then split up so they had to choose. The plan seemed to work. Once there were no other aircraft in sight we banked round and headed back towards our destination. It was only as we came in over the last of the trees that I realised we were heading for Roger's house. From above it was possible to see just how huge it was, and just how isolated, like a stack of glass boxes piling up the hill, a terrace above each one and a shimmering black swimming pool on the highest one.

Jo-Jo was already safely inside the house by the time we came in from the helipad at the top of the hill. She was sitting on a sofa with both the children huddled close. Roger was standing behind her, awkwardly kneading her shoulders with his enormous hands in a clumsy attempt at offering comfort. Now that he had started it didn't look like he knew how to disengage himself. Her parents lifted one child each as soon as they got to her.

"Let's go explore Roger's house," Martin said.

A houseboy appeared in the doorway.

"Show the kids where everything is and make them something to eat," Roger instructed him, sounding much as he would if talking to a computer.

Before they were quite out the door Jo-Jo stood up and came towards me, putting her arms around my chest and hugging as tightly as a small child, burying her face into my shirt. I could feel the sobs that were pressing her body against mine as she let loose everything she had been holding in. I caught Lillian's eye as she left the room, unable to read anything in her deadpan stare. Martin was too busy answering a flood of questions from Harvey, who must have been holding everything in up till now, perhaps instinctively knowing that his mother wasn't yet ready to talk. Roger was still standing behind the sofa, staring out of the window, drumming his fingers on the cushion and looking even more uncomfortable. It occurred to me that this was the first time I had seen him make any physical contact with another person beyond an overly firm, almost frantic, handshake. I wondered if he had ever been hugged. It was quite easy to imagine that he had not and that he would find the sight of someone else being hugged difficult to observe.

Then I forgot about Roger because all I could think was how wonderful her hair smelled beneath my face and how tiny her frame was when I put my arms around her and how totally reassuring an embrace from another human being can be. I rested my cheek on the top of her head and squeezed her, comforting myself as much as her, unable to stop the tears. There are some moments in life that you immediately know you are never going to forget.

None of us talked much that evening, concentrating on entertaining the children while surreptitiously following the story in the media. The silent staff provided food and the police came to the house to take my statement officially. They told me a little about the killer and his grudge against the superpowers of Silicon Valley, looking around them at the obvious extravagance of their surroundings with expressionless faces as they talked. Once the children had gone to bed, we channel-surfed openly, with Roger in control of the remote. The stories seemed to be everywhere and we learned about other friends of Roger's and Jo-Jo's who had children at the school, some of whose tiny bodies were now lying in the mortuary.

Chuck was by far the most famous casualty and more and more film of him kept appearing from the vaults of the media companies and photo libraries. The fact that he had been there to give his life to protect his children, while all the other fathers were not, was pointed out by a pundit and the quote kept reappearing on different bulletins, increasing his modern-man, hero status. There was news footage of us flying off the estate as well, looking for all the world like the opening credits of M*A*S*H, further muddying the divisions in viewers' minds between fact and fiction, war and comedy, social comment and entertainment. Who on earth could hope to work out what was real and what was fake any more?

Roger's phone buzzed constantly and most of the calls he rejected. My inbox was gradually filling up with messages from desperate publishers, now willing to offer virtually anything for a shot at the world's biggest story. In the past I would have felt nothing but exhilaration at being the recipient of so much attention, but that day I felt more like I was bobbing in an open sea, being circled by sharks.

Eventually fatigue overcame all of us and I went to the bedroom I had been allocated. I didn't do anything about blacking out the windows, wanting to be woken naturally by the sun rising over the mountains. I was on the verge of falling into a very deep sleep when I was aware of the door opening softly. There were barely audible footsteps and then I felt someone sitting on the side of the bed. Light fingers rested on my shoulder.

"Jo-Jo?" I whispered.

"I really need to be held," she said.

I lifted the sheets and allowed her to slide in beside me. She cuddled close, her scent filling my head again, her tiny arms gripping tightly as she cried herself to sleep.

16

෯ఆ

I must have slept particularly deeply that night because I didn't hear Jo-Jo leave the room and I had missed the sunrise by several hours when my eyes finally opened. Outside the window I could see a couple of helicopters circling in the clear blue sky. By the time I emerged into the living areas there were a lot of people already milling around. I recognised some of the television crew from Jo-Jo's house. It seemed they were being allowed to film everything that was going on. There was also a photographer, who I knew was famous for her news photographs and for spreads in magazines like *Vogue* and *Vanity Fair*. She was sitting with Roger at the breakfast bar as he brought up images on his tablet screen.

"Yeah," she said, with what to me sounded like a hint of impatience, "I get it, Roger, really I do."

I casually peered over his shoulder, just in time to see that he was bringing up iconic images of Jackie Kennedy and her two children at the funeral of their father, and the young sons of Princess Diana marching through London behind their mother's coffin.

Jo-Jo and her children were breakfasting at another table and I moved over to join them. When she greeted me she gave no indication that anything significant had passed between us during the night. I was partly relieved that there was nothing more to it than a gesture of friendship, partly disappointed that the magical moment seemed to have passed, and wholly confused about how I actually felt about any of it. For a moment I wondered if I had dreamt the whole thing and then I caught her scent as she leaned across to absent-mindedly wipe scarlet jam from Bette's face and I remembered the traces she had left on my pillow.

Both the children were quiet and solemn looking, their sad eyes constantly distracted by the people moving around them, flickering from one person to the next as if still hoping to come across their father. A cameraman was circling around the table and so I pulled back. I was pretty sure that the lawyers in London were not going to want me appearing anywhere in the televised version of the grieving family's life.

Grabbing a croissant and a cup of coffee I went out onto the terrace and sat looking at the view for a few moments, gathering my thoughts before I pulled out my silenced phone to check my messages. Every one of the publishers, who had contacted me a few days before, had sent another, more urgent message. There was also a long list of missed calls, sometimes several in a row from the same people. It seemed that Jo-Jo's autobiography had just quadrupled in potential value to the world's big publishers, and no one in the industry was now in any doubt that I was in California to write it.

I dropped the phone back into my pocket, not feeling up to dealing with any of them, wanting to spend more time sorting out my own thoughts and feelings. It seemed ironic that I should feel so reluctant to join in a game that most professional writers can only ever dream of being invited to play. In the past I had enjoyed the short periods when I had found myself in possession of a story that several different companies were willing to bid for competitively. Because of the size of the fee I was being paid this time, however, and because it seemed tawdry to be even thinking of capitalising on poor Chuck's demise and his family's broken hearts, I felt no urge to talk to any of them.

"Excuse me. Do you mind if we join you?"

I glanced up to find a couple, who looked to be in their early seventies, hovering nervously beside me. They both held themselves well, like strong, younger people, but their skins were weather beaten and lined with a mixture of sun and sadness.

"Of course not," I said, "please." I indicated the other seats around the low table. "I'm Andrew." I held out my hand.

The man shook my hand first, then the woman. Both had remarkably strong grips and their palms were hard and calloused from physical work.

"I'm Mick Huck," he said. "This is my wife, Sally." He paused for a few beats as if summoning the energy or courage to say something further. "Charlie was our son."

"Oh, I am so sorry." I instantly felt a surge of guilt. I had been so wrapped up in the grief of Jo-Jo and the kids that I had completely forgotten that Chuck must have other relatives who would be equally broken-hearted to lose him.

"We are told that you were the last person to talk to him," Mick continued after a few half-hearted comments on the beauty of the view spread below us, "that you were with him when ..."

"We wondered if you would be kind enough to tell us exactly what happened," his wife took over, seeing that he was having trouble getting the words out. They were both staring at me intently, as if I was the last link they had with their lost son.

"Of course," I said. "Whatever you want to know."

"Well," he glanced nervously at his wife, who gripped his liver-spotted hand tightly with her own, "I think we would like to know everything."

They remained holding hands all through my description of the trip to the school, the shootings and Chuck's last brave moments, their eyes unwaveringly fixed on mine.

"Does Charlie have any brothers or sisters?" I asked.

"No," Mick said.

"I wasn't able to have any more," Sally interrupted, "but I didn't mind because we were happy just to have him. He was just a ray of sunshine in our lives, always so happy and always so helpful. A true gift from God."

"We have a small farm," Mick explained, "and Charlie used to help me all the time, until he came out to California to be an actor."

"You must have missed him a lot," I said, wishing I had my tape machine with me, but knowing this was definitely not the moment to go and get it.

"Oh yes," Sally said, "so much. But you have to let your children go, don't you? And look at the wonderful grandchildren he gave us."

I followed her stare back through the doors into the room, which seemed so full of people, to the two children staring vacantly up at the adults talking around them.

"It was good to see him on the television after he left home," Mick said. "We could see that he was having a great time, and then he met Jo-Jo." He fell silent.

"She's a great mother," I said.

"Of course," Sally said. "We haven't been able to get to know her as much as we would have liked. She's so busy and we don't get out to California very often ..."

"It's hard to leave a farm," Mick explained, "but Charlie used to bring the kids over to visit us whenever Jo-Jo was away filming."

"They love it on the farm," Sally said, smiling despite the tears welling up.

"How did you get here today?" I asked.

"Mr Rex sent a plane for us," she said.

"There were so many reporters and film crews coming out to the farm," Mick explained, "we were afraid we might say the wrong thing and end up all over the front pages. You know what the media are like with their fake news." He suddenly stopped himself. "I'm sorry; you're a journalist, aren't you?"

"No," I laughed, "no. I'm a ghostwriter. A very different thing."

"A ghostwriter?" Mick looked puzzled and I remembered my presence there was supposed to be a secret.

"I write books," I said, "not newspapers."

"Andrew," Roger's huge hand gripped my shoulder unexpectedly from behind, making me jump and pinning me down at the same time, unnerving me in a way I couldn't explain. "I'm going for a walk. Care to join me? There are some great views."

17

ഔഇ

If keeping up with Roger's strides in Park Lane had been hard, ascending the hills of Los Altos with him was torture, but I was determined not to complain or fall back.

"Good people," he said as I trotted beside him. "Mick and Sally are good people. That needs to come across in the book. Jo-Jo bonded with them right from the beginning. Decent, upright, hard-working, God-fearing folk. The back bone of America and they were happy to welcome a mixed-race girl into their family. Wonderful people."

"Jo-Jo hasn't mentioned them much so far," I admitted, "and they told me they don't really know her ..."

"Ask her about them when you next have some one-on-one time with her," he continued as if he hadn't heard me. "She'll tell you how much she respects them and their values and the way they brought Chuck up. It was their values that made him the stand-up decent guy he was. She'll tell you that. She would want the same for her kids."

"Okay," I said. "I'll ask her about them. We haven't really talked about the wedding and family side of things yet."

"Great." He paused and threw his arms wide, taking a deep breath, "Just look at that view, Andrew! Isn't it great? Doesn't it make you glad to be alive just looking at it? What a sky!"

"It's a beautiful place," I agreed. "You are very lucky."

"I am," he said, as if realising it for the first time. "I am, aren't I? Fantastic time to be alive, fantastic country to be alive in."

He fell unusually silent for a moment and I got the impression he was trying to think of the best way to say something difficult. I said nothing, enjoying the opportunity to catch my breath and admire the view.

"She really likes you," he said eventually, still staring into the distance. "Jo-Jo really likes you. She says she feels like the two of you must have known each other in a previous life."

"Really?"

"She has a great spiritual side, a bit of the Confucius thing from her mother, I guess, and some of the old Mayan stuff from her dad. A mix of deep spiritual beliefs. She feels you have connected. She said that. I can see that. She's leaning on you spiritually."

"Glad to hear it," I said, partly because I genuinely was glad, and partly because I wanted to give him a chance to stop rambling so uncomfortably and change the subject.

"Great job," he continued. "You have done a really great job of winning her trust. I can see how the two of you are bonding. It's just great. So great to have you on board."

"Good." It was nice to hear this but I had a feeling the praise was leading somewhere less agreeable.

"We have a great relationship, Jo-Jo and me," he said, setting off up the hill again. "She tells me everything, you know. I always insist on that with anyone I go into business with. Complete trust and transparency is so important when you are in partnership with someone."

"Partnership?"

"That's what we are in danger of losing in the West," he said, still ignoring my interjections. "Trust. If people don't trust their leaders and their politicians and their celebrities then the whole edifice is likely to fall to pieces, the whole of society. We all need heroes and heroines, people to look up to ..."

"How exactly does your partnership with Jo-Jo work?" I tried a direct question, raising my voice a little to overcome my returning breathlessness and to make it harder for him to ignore me.

"We've been in a lot of investments together," he said. "You know all about that. I've been totally open with you about that; totally transparent. She's a great business woman, really great. A fantastic eye for the ways things are going, spotting the trends, seeing what's coming, what's going to be the next big thing. She's great. I think she has enormous potential, huge, not just as a film star, not just reality television. She could be something really big, really important. You must have spotted that, just from the amount of time you have spent with her."

"Lillian gave me some of the essays she wrote when she was young," I said, "I have to admit they are pretty impressive."

"Great. I'm glad Lillian did that. So you can see the level of intelligence we are dealing with here. The spiritual depths. All that needs to come out in the book."

"I gather Lillian wanted to match you two up ..."

He said nothing, just kept walking and staring at the view. I wasn't sure if he had heard. Eventually he spoke.

"Lillian believes she knows what's best for everyone. She believes she can make things happen just because she thinks they should. She's a great mother, really great. She's a great wife for Martin. He couldn't have achieved half the things he has achieved without her help. She's the greatest fund raiser ever, really great. She can make almost anything happen if she puts her mind to it."

"So did you and Jo-Jo ever think of getting together, like she wanted?"

The question seemed to floor him, leaving him as embarrassed and awkward as a twelve-year-old boy accused of fancying a grown woman.

"It's hard to find the time for everything you want to do in life," he said, increasing his pace, as if trying to get away from my questions.

I stopped talking for a while, partly because I needed

all the oxygen I could get as the incline beneath our feet grew steeper, and partly because I felt some conflicting emotions. I couldn't work out what Roger's real feelings were towards Jo-Jo, but I was beginning to suspect that he was in love, or as near as he could manage, even if he didn't realise it himself. The thought of them having any sort of relationship ignited a small flame of jealousy somewhere in the depths of my soul, which I was anxious to snuff out as quickly as possible. I needed some time on my own to think about everything he was telling me, and to work out what it was that he obviously wasn't telling me. I needed to rationalise my own feelings and get back to just listening to the story and trying to understand what it was Jo-Jo was going to want to say in this book, not what Roger thought she wanted to say.

As the view across his property grew ever more pan-oramic I noticed that there were small groups of people at each of the gates and on the tops of each hill. Those that were close enough for me to see clearly had the look of security guards. It was beginning to feel as if we really had been brought here for our protection and that we were somewhat imprisoned – albeit in a sort of paradise.

"I've given a lot of thought to what you were saying about selecting a publisher," he continued eventually, apparently not remotely out of breath, his strides just as long as when we set out. "I would like you to keep talking unofficially to all the publishers who have shown an interest. Get them to come out here if they're willing. Let's hear what they have to offer."

"Okay," I said cautiously. "I don't have much experience in negotiating ..."

"That's okay. If we decide to go with them the lawyers will take care of that. I would also like to get your wife's views on the project. You said she did this sort of thing."

"She does," I paused to take in the view and get my breath back again. He had continued several strides before realising he was alone and turned back. "Would you like me to ask her if she would be interested in packaging the book for you?"

"Let's get her out here."

"When?"

"Now. We'll take care of everything. I'll email her."

"We have a young daughter."

"I know. She can bring her. It will be a distraction for Jo-Jo's kids, someone new to play with."

"You can ask her," I said, doubtfully. I didn't have any memory of telling Roger about Maddy. How did he know so much? "Do you want her email?"

"I have it."

"You do?"

He had returned to walking and my mind was racing as I tried to catch up. How come he had Caroline's email? I had certainly not given it to him. He must have googled her and found her website. When did he do that? After he saw Jo-Jo hugging me? I wasn't sure how I felt about him stalking my wife in the dead of night. I told myself to get a grip. I often checked people out, why wouldn't he do the same? Would Caroline be willing to just drop everything and fly out here with Maddy? I was slightly nervous at the prospect of being responsible for making sure they were both comfortable and happy while I was still concentrating most of my mind on getting the story out of Jo-Jo and her family. I was also not sure how she would react to the closeness I now seemed to have with Jo-Jo.

"She's American, right?" Roger called over his shoulder.

"Yes."

"So, no problem with visas or anything. It will be really great to meet her, and nice for you to have your family here. Doesn't this mountain air smell fantastic? Everyone is going to be pretty tied up with planning for the funeral over the next few days so you may find you have time on your hands. You can show her all this." He spread his long arms out to their full extent, turning three hundred and sixty degrees to take in everything below, bringing to mind the statue of Christ the Redeemer looking down over the city of Rio de Janeiro – or was it Julie Andrews in the opening credits of *The Sound of Music*?

"Okay." I said, doubtfully, not at all sure how this was going to pan out. Everything was moving too fast for me to fully take it in or to exercise any control over its outcome.

18

ജ

When we got back to the house there seemed to be activity everywhere. Jo-Jo was being filmed with a fashion designer on one of the terraces, deciding on the outfit she would be wearing for the funeral, watched over by the chain-smoking *Vanity Fair* photographer, and the kids were in the pool with Chuck's parents, neither of them showing any signs of their usual high spirits. I was informed by a houseboy that there were two agents from the FBI waiting to talk to me in one of the "living studios", as Roger liked to call them.

Roger disappeared into his office, pursued by Julia, who seemed to have a number of people on her phone, all waiting for a chance to speak to him urgently.

The two agents introduced themselves but I didn't take in their names. Neither of them appeared even remotely friendly. I guessed they had been waiting some time. They looked incongruously smart in their suits, ties and shiny black leather shoes.

"Are you okay?" the older one asked as I poured myself a glass of water and sank into one of the low white sofas.

"Absolutely," I assured them. "I've just been for a walk with Mr Rex and he sets a pace I'm not used to."

Neither of them smiled. "You and Mr Rex are good friends then?"

"Not really. He's hired me."

"Hired you?"

"To write a book. I'm an author."

I tried to sound vague, aware that I was an unconvincing liar at the best of times and that these men were trained specifically to sniff out untruths. I had no idea if the contract I had signed forbade me from even telling the FBI the real reason I was there. I was aware from the newspaper headlines of recent years that the FBI took a dim view of people who withheld information from them, but I was even more afraid of how Roger's London lawyers would react if they thought I had betrayed them.

"We were told you were writing a book about Jo-Jo Win," the younger one said, consulting his notes.

"Who told you that?" I asked.

"She did."

"Okay. I've signed a lot of confidentiality agreements," I said, "I need to check what I am allowed to say and not say."

"Are you saying that you want to bring a lawyer in to

this conversation, Mr Crofts?" The older man narrowed his eyes and leaned in close as if wanting to read my mind.

"No, God, no. I'm just not sure what I am allowed to talk about."

I was aware that I was now sweating even more than when I came in from the walk. Why did talking to policemen always make me feel so guilty, even when I hadn't done anything wrong?

"We'll keep this talk off the record then," the agent said, leaning back and smiling in a way that made it clear he wasn't actually amused. "So what exactly is Mr Rex's role in Jo-Jo Win's life?"

"I think they're good friends," I said, realising as I said it just how lame it sounded, "and they are business partners. Why?"

He ignored my question. "They must be very good friends," the agent mused, "because he seems to be putting himself out a great deal here." He gestured at the crowd of people we could see moving about on the terraces on the other side of the wide picture windows.

"Yeah," I took a sip of water, aware of what he was insinuating and being careful not to say anything that they might repeat to either Jo-Jo or Roger. "I think they are."

"Can I ask you," the agent continued, changing his tone to sound as if we were having a normal conversation, "off the record, of course; was everything okay with Mr Huck and Miss Win's marriage? Were there any tensions?"

"No," I felt I could be pretty certain of my facts here.

"They seemed completely devoted and united over bringing up the kids. Why?" I was genuinely interested to know why they would ask such a question.

"It's just routine questions," the younger one said, gazing out of the window at the vista beyond. "We have to check out the situations for all the victims of the shooting, in case there is a motive we might be overlooking."

"Really?" I was shocked. "I thought the guy was a nutter with a grudge. Didn't he make a video about how he hated the rich?"

"Yeah, yeah, sure, sure," the older one said, "it's just routine. You know what it's like with police work, especially when it comes to high-profile victims. There are going to be a million conspiracy theories out there on the internet, we need to make sure that we haven't missed anything obvious. We don't want to end up looking dumb."

"You and Charlie Huck were buddies then?" the other one chipped in.

"I've only known him a week or so. We had hung out a bit, mainly with the kids. He was a nice guy."

"So everyone tells us." Both agents fell silent for a moment. "So, no reason you can think of why a killer might want to target him?"

"No, absolutely not." My head was spinning. I couldn't get my mind round the things that they were inferring. "Everyone liked him. He was just part of the collateral damage, wasn't he?"

"I gather you have been a great comfort to Ms Win," the older man said, almost absent-mindedly.

"I'm sorry?"

"We're told it was you she turned to first for comfort yesterday ..."

"Who told you that?"

Neither of them answered; both just looking at me with their dead eyes.

"She just needed to be held by someone," I said, feeling myself blushing like a kid.

Suddenly we were back to shaking hands like we were winding up a formal business meeting. It was unnerving to be the object of so much direct eye contact after spending time with Roger, who gave out virtually none. I hoped I was giving no indication as to how shaken up I was feeling by the entire encounter. Was that the effect they had intended to achieve? Were they suggesting that Jo-Jo and I had somehow planned Chuck's murder?

They left the room and I sat down for a few minutes, sipping water, staring at the hills that I had recently been walking on, trying to collect my thoughts. When I finally pulled myself together I made my way to the bedroom I had been designated and Skyped Caroline, aware that it would be late in the evening for her.

"Hi," she said and I could tell from her voice that she was aware something was up.

"Hi," I said. "Just to warn you, I think you're going to get an email from Roger Rex."

"Already had it," she grinned, "and a phone call."

"Sorry," I said, "I meant to warn you first, so you would be prepared. I didn't think he would be that fast off the mark."

"Don't be sorry. Maddy and I could do with a bit of California sunshine. Why should you have all the fun?"

"You're coming out?"

"He makes it very hard to say no. It would be fun to work together on something again after all this time. As long as it's okay with you."

"Of course, why wouldn't it be okay with me?"

"I know how involved you become with your authors." I felt myself blushing again and hoped she wouldn't notice. "I don't want to distract you and give you something else to worry about when you're trying to concentrate on getting the story."

"It's not a problem for me. I just wasn't sure that you would want to, with all the work you have on."

"Too good an opportunity to miss, don't you think? I promise to stay out of your way if you're working."

"He wants me to find out what the big publishers are going to offer too."

"I know. He said. He won't go with any of them."

"How can you be so confident?"

"Why would he pay for me to come all the way out to the West Coast unless he intended to hire me? And if he's as comfortable with you as he says he is, then why wouldn't he let us handle the whole thing together? Like you said, he's a control freak. If he uses us he keeps complete control of everything."

"They'll all be willing to offer millions – even more now than a few days ago."

"He doesn't need millions. Neither does she, does she?"

"No, I guess not."

"See you in a couple of days then. Got to go, packing to do. Love you. Can't wait to see you."

19

ೞಲ

"The President has expressed a wish to come to the funeral."

Roger made the announcement to a full room while everyone was eating lunch.

"The President of the United States?" Chuck's mother asked, clutching at her husband's hand for support. The rest of the room remained quiet. The cameraman kept filming, moving from Roger to Jo-Jo.

"It is very kind of the President to express his sympathies," Jo-Jo said, as if choosing each word individually, staring hard at the slice of pizza in her hand. "But I would like to make it very clear that no politician will be welcome at this ceremony unless they are on the record as supporting gun control and have no record of receiving money from the NRA."

"But the President," Chuck's father said after a few

moments. "The President of the United States wants to come to Charlie's funeral, Jo-Jo."

She looked across at her parents-in-law. "It is a great compliment to Charlie, Mick, a great compliment. But if the gun laws were different this maniac might never have been able to do what he did and Charlie would still be with us."

Tears rose in Sally's eyes. "You must do what you think is right, Jo-Jo," she said, squeezing her husband's hand as if to quieten him. "You understand these things. But it was good of the President to make that gesture."

Roger murmured something to Julia who disappeared into another room with the cameraman. A few minutes later Jo-Jo's announcement about gun control and about the President being unwelcome at the service was online and starting to go viral.

I moved over to sit beside Roger. "The President was willing to fly all the way out here from Washington?"

"His people would have advised it," Roger said, typing into his phone as he talked and chewing pizza at the same time. "He would want to be seen consoling Jo-Jo at this difficult time. She has a big following and they are the sort of people he really needs to win over."

"Will he take this rejection personally?"

"I would imagine," Roger took another slice of pizza. "But Jo-Jo has no obligation to provide him with any oxygen."

"Oxygen?"

"The Oxygen of Publicity. A phrase your Lady Thatcher used about terrorism. Have you tried this pizza? This is such great pizza; you should try it, really! Jo-Jo felt very strongly about gun control, even before this."

Later, sitting on a terrace with the tape machine running and the camera team gone to bed, I asked Jo-Jo when she first formed such strong feelings about gun control. She lit a cigarette.

"This is off the record, right?" I went to switch off the machine. "No, I mean the cigarette. I don't smoke. The kids would kill me if they thought I did."

"I see no cigarette."

She nodded and smiled for the first time in two days. "When you are a little girl," she said after a few moments, "and you are living in a strange, hot country, where there doesn't appear to be any law or order, and big men come out of the jungle in the middle of the night carrying big guns and wake you up and shout at you a lot and fire rounds into the trees, that makes a serious impression."

"Where was this?"

"The Congo, I think. We can check the dates. My father would remember. They gave him a very hard time that night. I was old enough to be able to remember very clearly how frightening it felt. And I also remember the looks on the faces of the people who had the guns, and the looks on the faces of those who didn't. My feelings on the subject have not changed since that night."

"But all those movies you made, where you shot everyone in sight."

"Yeah," she said. "I guess my worldly ambitions at that time were stronger than my scruples. If I could I would have them all withdrawn from circulation, but then that would not fit easily with my beliefs about freedom of speech and freedom of expression. I am as strongly against any kind of censorship as I am against unregulated gun-ownership. Things become more complicated as you grow older, don't you find?"

She fell quiet for a while, sucking the smoke deep into her lungs. The songs of the night insects were the only sound going into the recorder.

"Thanks for being there for me," she said eventually.

"No problem."

"No, really. It was a big help having an actual shoulder to cry on." She reached over and squeezed my hand.

"It was the least I could do."

"I hear your wife is coming out," she said, still holding my hand.

"Yeah."

"Checking up on you?" she teased.

"I doubt it. She is the most secure woman you could ever hope to meet."

"She sounded pretty incredible in the 'Italian Gardener' book."

"She is."

"Was it my mother's idea to ask her out?"

"I don't know," I was genuinely surprised by the suggestion. "Why would she want to do that?"

"She doesn't like other people getting too close to me. She never really took to Chuck."

"I thought it was Roger's idea, but I don't know."

"Yeah," she nodded. "That makes sense. Poor old Roger."

"You'll like her," I said. "You should get her to publish the book for you. She's fun to work with."

"I'm sure I will like her. You need to talk to Roger about the publishing side."

"I already have. Or rather, he's talked to me."

She laughed, finally releasing my hand, which made me feel a tiny bit sad, and lying back in the chair, staring up at the stars. "He's something else, isn't he? He's been very good to us as a family. Dad wouldn't have been able to get half as many projects up and running without his backing. I certainly wouldn't have made as much money investing in the tech industries. He's a good guy." It sounded like she was trying to convince herself as much as me.

"I gather your mother thought you should date him."

"My mother has a lot of strange ideas," she laughed. "But he is a really good guy."

The following day the Tesla delivered a tired looking Caroline and a sleeping Maddy to the house. Jo-Jo embraced Caroline like she was a long-lost sister and the kids immediately wanted to wake Maddy up so that they could play with her.

20

⚛

Roger was right about the President taking the rejection personally, but he could hardly attack the nation's sweetheart days after she had been tragically widowed. Others were not so squeamish. The online world seemed to divide almost equally between those who applauded her stand against guns – and her slap to the face of the leader of the free world – and those who saw it as evidence that she was Satan in female form.

However, the people who were ranting and raving online – mostly in capital letters – appeared not to be the sort of people who would actually turn out on the streets with banners, chanting angry slogans. The crowd that formed around Grace Cathedral a few days later seemed to be entirely respectful of the newly bereaved widow and her family. Many of them actually seemed to be grieving for someone they felt they had known personally. Maybe those who were most vociferous online in defence of guns just didn't come from the San Francisco area. On all the surrounding roofs I could see police snipers watching the crowd.

The only banners in evidence were enlarged pictures of Chuck from his beach-boy, soap opera heyday. Many of the same pictures were also being disported on the t-shirts of women taking their first steps into middle age, and a fair number of men.

"Did Chuck have any idea he had this many fans?" I asked Jo-Jo as we were ushered into the cathedral through the weeping and wailing crowd.

"Yeah," she smiled sweetly at the memory, "he knew all right. All those millions of posters they printed up of him, showing off on the beach without his shirt, had to have ended up on someone's bedroom walls."

* * *

Caroline had offered to stay back at Roger's house with the children, but Roger had insisted that Harvey and Bette should come to the service. They were both dressed in impossibly cute black outfits, looking around them with wide-eyed terror at the wet-eyed crowd pressing in from every side behind the police cordons, each clinging to one of their mother's hands. I was glad that Maddy was not being subjected to the noise of the crowd but I wished Caroline was there to help me with the star spotting. Some politicians from the gun-control end of the spectrum, like the Obamas, had managed to get into the service and there were some of the more famous faces from Silicon Valley, but the vast majority of the seats were taken up by the great and the good of Hollywood. It looked more like a night out at the Oscars than a religious service. Having only seen Jo-Jo in her own home or in Roger's home, I had forgotten just how big a player she was in the film, television and video games industries. This was a people turning out to pay homage to their queen.

Roger was stage-managing everything, albeit via Julia and her ear-piece. The service went smoothly, televised live all over the world, but then they had to control the re-emergence of the coffin and mourners into the crowds. The million dollar shot had to be of Jo-Jo and the children coming out onto the cathedral steps behind the coffin. The deafening rattle from the firing squad of cameras seemed to go on forever as the little family walked sadly towards the waiting limousines. The four grandparents were already being ushered into their vehicles by Julia, who was still wearing a headset and talking continually to someone on the other end. All the photographers, apart from one, were being held back by a chain of police in full riot-gear. The one exception was the *Vanity Fair* photographer Roger had been briefing at the house, the one who had been present at the dress-fitting. She seemed to have some sort of special pass, allowing her to get in as close to the family with her lenses as she wanted to, even allowing her to smoke at moments when no one else in the entourage would have dared.

Without telling anyone where I was going, I slipped through the crowd and walked the few blocks to the Ritz-Carlton. It was a relief to escape the noise and the crush of bodies onto open sidewalks. The hotel looked pretty much like a cathedral itself; a temple to the gods of luxury and super-convenience. Giles was ensconced in a red leather armchair in the lounge, reading on his tablet. Afternoon tea was laid out on the table in front of him. He looked like he had lost weight since he last bought me lunch. I guessed some late mid-life health scare had forced him to join a gym.

"Is this okay?" he asked, gesturing to the tea, "or would you prefer something stronger?"

"No, this is fine." I sank into a matching chair. "That was a heck of a circus."

"I watched a bit of the television coverage in the room before I came down."

"Do you remember that scene in *Day of the Locust*, where the crowd at a Hollywood premiere runs amok and ends up burning down the city? Crowds like that always make me nervous."

"The star of the show handled herself well, I thought."

"She's a class act. Really. Far cooler in every way than I ever expected."

"We think so," he said, pouring me a cup of tea and indicating that I should help myself from the cake stand. "Everyone in the office is really excited about the project.

That's why I was keen to come out and pitch to you personally. We really want this book, Andrew."

"You know the final decision won't be up to me, don't you?"

"We would really like to have a chance to pitch direct to her if you can arrange it."

"I'm not even sure it's her you need to convince. Roger Rex seems to be the mastermind behind this whole thing."

"Really? That's interesting. How come?"

"Not completely sure. The two of them seem to have fingers in many of the same pies, business-wise. He's very keen to make this book huge."

"That would be our aim too. Are there many others in the race?"

"Everyone is in the race, but Roger is also pretty keen on the idea of self-publishing."

"Really? Jesus Christ." He was obviously shocked and for a moment he said nothing, chewing on a sandwich while he thought. "You know, when I started in this business there was no such thing as 'self-publishing'. It was called 'vanity publishing' and the only people who fell for it were those who couldn't get a real publishing deal. It was considered a con, perpetrated on gullible would-be writers."

"Plenty of famous writers down the ages started out by paying to publish themselves," I reminded him " – Virginia Wolf, Beatrix Potter, Mark Twain, Margaret

Atwood ... Writers like to keep control of their work and now that it is affordable ..."

"Yes, I know all the arguments," he stopped, realising he had snapped at the person most likely to get him into the presence of Jo-Jo and Roger. "Sorry. It's just exasperating. We have more than a century of experience ..."

"Someone like Roger can buy all that experience in. He has more money at his disposal than most small countries. He can afford to hire editors and designers. He can afford to print the book. He can afford to put an entire marketing team onto selling it – a publisher will have to come up with a really good reason for him to hand over all that control – not to mention the percentages and royalties."

"We can always negotiate over the royalties," Giles said, regaining his composure, "and we could give Roger or Jo-Jo, or anyone they like to nominate, the final veto over everything. What we can offer is to take away all the hassle and we can put down a substantial advance offer for world rights. I mean *really* substantial ... seven figures."

"There have been quite a lot of seven figure advances," I said, doubtfully.

"Not that many, surely."

"Well publishers' publicity departments do put out a lot of hype and misinformation, I know that," I admitted. "But it's been reported that a number of people have had up to ten million."

"This offer wouldn't be hype," he assured me, refilling his teacup. "This would be actual money in the bank."

"I think it would have to be eight figures at least to catch Roger's attention," I said, "and by that I mean sterling, not dollars."

"Well," he sat back and paused, obviously for dramatic purposes, "that's not impossible. But we would want some guarantees that you aren't talking to anyone else."

"I'm not in a position to give anyone any guarantees about anything," I laughed, "I'm just the ghost, remember? And Roger Rex is the loosest cannon I have ever encountered."

"I bumped into your wife and daughter on the flight out," he casually changed the subject. "Only briefly, of course, because they were travelling in first class ..."

"You weren't in first class, Giles?" I teased.

"I have shareholders," he raised his eyebrows as if that explained everything. "Publishing is not as profitable as it used to be. Well ... obviously it is for you."

I shrugged, unable to deny that things seemed to be going well. I wondered if he remembered as keenly as I did the many pitches I had made in his office over the years, most of which had ended up rejected, or rewarded with offers so miniscule I would end up working at about half the minimum wage. I doubted it. I also knew that he must have guessed why Caroline was being brought out to California in such style.

"She's hardly changed since I first met her," Giles went on. "Still beautiful."

When Caroline had first arrived in London she had served briefly as Giles's assistant, moving on to work for a small publisher called Arnold Petteridge after a few months, when she discovered it was impossible to exist in a modern city on the sort of wages that the big publishers paid.

"And Maddy was just adorable."

"Thanks," I said, helping myself to a small, pink macaroon.

21

ಶ್ರೀ ಚ

Caroline and Roger were drinking their way through a pot of coffee when I got back to the house, Maddy having been taken off by Bette and Harvey, who informed me they were playing "mummies and daddies" with her as I passed them on my way in. She seemed extremely content with the attention so I left them to it.

"Your wife is great," Roger enthused as I brought myself a cup to the table. "Really great!"

"I know," I said, pleased to see that Caroline looked a little abashed by the forthright compliment. Over the years she had grown used to living with British irony.

"Did you have your meeting?" Roger asked as he flicked around the internet on his phone, mainly bringing up pictures of Jo-Jo and the children walking behind the coffin. It seemed that he had got exactly the iconic images he had hoped for.

"I did. They are very keen. They will pretty much pay

whatever you ask. I mentioned eight figures and he didn't back down."

"Giles offered eight figures?" Caroline said. "They must really believe the book has potential. They don't give away money like that unless they think they will get it back. Not any more."

"That's what I thought. He also really doesn't want any of his rivals to get it."

"That's great news," Roger refilled his cup. "How soon can we have a first draft to look at?"

"A couple of months. I could do a first draft of about forty thousand words. If you're happy with that I would probably be able to show you another forty thousand a couple of months after that."

"That's great." He turned back to Caroline. "And how soon could you be getting some cover designs done?"

It seemed they had got further in their discussions than I had realised. It seemed Caroline had been right in her prediction and Giles had wasted his time and money on the trip to San Francisco. Illogically, I felt sorry for him.

"Soon as you want," she said. "I could be asking designers to start work right now, if you like."

"That's great. That's really great. So we could have a book ready for the shops in six months?"

"Sure," Caroline winked at me. "Bet Giles didn't promise that, did he?"

"I doubt he'd be comfortable with that sort of timeline,"

I laughed, "but the mood he was in, I think he would currently agree to anything."

"We don't need them," Roger said, like it was a final decision. "Why would anyone need them any more? The concept of the middle-man is so twentieth century."

For a second I wondered how long it would be before people like Roger didn't even need writers any more. Surely a clever algorithm could put together a novel or a film script as easily as a CGI department could put together an actor.

I was pretty sure I had enough material recorded but I did two more days of interviewing before flying back to England with Caroline and Maddy.

"Exciting times," Caroline said as we sat at the bar in the first class area, Maddy having fallen asleep the moment the plane took off.

"Indeed."

"Have you been keeping a diary?"

"I have. Partly to remind myself of everything that happened and everything that was said, and partly to fill in the evenings when no one was free to talk. But I can't imagine I will ever be allowed to publish."

"Who knows? Things are changing so fast," she sipped her gin and tonic. "Things that were state secrets yesterday are twitter-fodder tomorrow."

"Very profound."

"Thank you. I have to go up to London to sign all the relevant contracts with Roger's lawyers next week."

"Okay. Just let me know which day and I'll make sure I'm at home."

"I think I can combine it with Maddy going for a play-day, so you'll probably just need to drop her off and pick her up."

"Whatever you need."

I was beginning to feel the familiar anxiety building inside my head as to whether I would be able to find enough hours to get the book written to the deadline I had promised Roger, but I knew Caroline was under just as much pressure, needing to clear all her other projects out the way to make room for this.

"Giles is going to be really pissed off that you got him all the way out there for nothing," she continued.

"I never made any promises," I said, feeling another pang of guilt.

"He's still going to be pissed off."

"I know, but he'll be retiring soon. He's not enjoying the business any more."

"Did you understand everything that Roger's techie guys were saying about sending material back and forth?"

"Not completely. I guess they are going to be bringing me into the twenty-first century."

22

৪)৩

The same PC tower had been standing on my desk for at least ten years, probably more, reliably firing up each morning, much like the boiler that heated the water for our daily showers. I was also aware that my user system was falling behind the times because it kept issuing me dire little warnings about no longer being able to accept "updates", and various functions seemed to have stopped working. Since the word processing and emailing functions were fine, I had been soldiering on, frankly terrified that if I updated it I would lose something or be unable to continue operating the new system without thinking, as I had become used to doing for so long. For things like Skyping I could use a tablet anyway and Caroline, being far braver about such things than me, had her own state-of-the-art equipment which virtually published entire books from start to finish, so she could come to my rescue if someone asked for something that I did not feel confident to handle – things like "scanning documents" and "spreadsheets". I guess I was the new version of the generation of writers that insisted on continuing to write with fountain pens rather than transferring to typewriters – or even to biros. I was in danger of becoming a dinosaur way before the date for my extinction was due but, unlike the dinosaurs, I was at least aware of the approaching dangers.

So, when Roger sent people to the house with new shiny-black equipment for me, I knew I had to bite the bullet. I had no idea if my old computer was secure and if someone hacked in and stole material belonging to Jo-Jo I could be in serious legal trouble if I had refused his offer to take care of everything. Needless to say, the new equipment was not just beautiful, it was also easy to work on and within a day I was wondering why I had put off updating everything for so long.

I went through all the recordings I had done in California, typing up anything interesting any of the interviewees had said which I thought likely to make its way into the final book. I also worked on my own memories of the time spent there; building up the diary idea, as Caroline had suggested when the first email arrived from Roger, requesting a meeting in London. It had been such an intense few weeks, so full of new experiences and emotions that I wanted to record it all anyway, while it was all still fresh in my memory. I suppose it did occur to me that a diary might one day be a document of historical interest, perhaps even of monetary value, but that wasn't at the front of my mind because we had no money troubles at all thanks to Roger's payments into my bank account.

Nervous that I might press a delete button in error on the new, unfamiliar technology, I would email myself the works-in-progress at the end of each day, so that I knew that if I did have some sort of accident I could always go back to my email and find the most up-to-date versions of the works.

The great danger of being "connected" to the internet while writing is the temptation to have a peek at what might be happening in "real time" on social media. What stories are trending? What's the gossip? Tempting click bait lies in wait for the unwary web traveller at every turn. This temptation is increased a hundredfold when you are involved in the world's hottest story. The number of conspiracy theories circulating around Chuck's death was multiplying daily and although Jo-Jo had, by and large, acquired the status of a saint in the eyes of the majority, she was not immune to the back-stairs speculations. There were even theorists who believed that she and Roger had somehow plotted together and the whole playground bloodbath had been staged simply to muddy the waters around Chuck's exe-cution. The more outlandish the suggestions became the more I was hooked to read further, sucked inevitably into the dark world of millions of people's hyper-active imaginations and sick fantasies.

* * *

It was while enjoying the mild titillation of surfing through the latest of these nonsense stories that I was suddenly engulfed in a wave so huge and so terrifying I thought for a moment I was going to drown in my own adrenaline. Maybe that's not the best simile to describe how it felt. Maybe it was more like one of those car crashes where you are motoring happily along, maybe listening to your favourite tune and enjoying the sunshine, when you are suddenly hit broadside by a vehicle you did not see coming and your whole world seems to explode. Either way I felt simultaneously shocked and sick, unable to completely take in the full horror of what was happening on the screen in front of me.

It started with me coming across a Tweet, which referred to some item about Jo-Jo Win being in bed with her ghostwriter the day after her husband's assassination. They were quoting my own words from the diary – the first draft of this manuscript, containing virtually everything that you have been reading. That caused my heart to skip a beat. As I drilled further into the story, even seeing an aerial shot of Roger's house with my bedroom window circled, I began to find it hard to breathe and the nausea spread. I remembered, with another juddering shot of nausea, that I had decided to leave the curtains open that night and that there had been helicopters circling in the sky outside when I woke up. How good were those infra-red cameras they used to film wildlife at night? Would they work from that distance?

My first thought was; how do I shut this story down fast? But within seconds I had realised there was no chance of that happening. Then I wondered how I could steer Caroline away from seeing it. That thought was also no more than fleeting. Once a story like this starts to pick up speed there is no chance of stopping it reaching the eyes of someone connected to it. Within a few minutes of discovering the first clue that the story was out there I had realised that the next thing I had to do was to go talk to her. I found her in the garden. She was pushing Maddy in her swing, but her attention was almost a hundred per cent on her phone screen.

"My computer has been hacked," I said. "Everything has gone online."

She looked up and nodded, signifying that she had already worked that out. She had turned pale and her lips had grown so thin they had almost disappeared.

"They've taken one incident entirely out of context," I said, realising how lame and naïve my explanation sounded.

She gestured for me to take over pushing the swing so she could walk a few feet away and finish reading. I said nothing, attending to Maddy's questions about why the sky was blue and not pink, a colour she thought she would like much better. After what seemed like an age Caroline came back, still cradling the phone in her palm.

"Was this from the diary you were keeping?"

"Yes."

"Did anything else happen that you haven't recorded?"

"No."

"Promise?"

"Absolutely."

She took over pushing the swing again, lost in thought. I remembered how uncommunicative she had become after Becky's accident and I dreaded a return to that silence. Maddy seemed to sense the importance of the moment and stopped talking too. Eventually Caroline spoke again.

"So, she's actually become your guilty little pleasure after all."

I smiled, cautiously, not sure if I was yet on safe enough ground to turn the subject matter into banter. I had done nothing to be ashamed of, technically, I was sure of that, but I had waxed fairly lyrical in the diary entry about the scent of Jo-Jo's hair and the pleasures to be gained from a comforting hug.

"You need to find out where you stand legally," she said, her tone businesslike, although her eyes still seemed out of focus as if looking at something very far away. "The lawyers are bound to be pulling out the nondisclosure agreement and scanning the small print to see if they can sue."

Another wave of sickness buffeted me. I had been so overwhelmed by the personal embarrassment of the revelation I hadn't even thought of that potential side effect of this disaster.

"But the material was stolen, and Roger's people did all the security settings on the computer they gave me to work on. I can hardly be held responsible if some clever hacker managed to get round them."

"You'll need a lawyer's opinion on that."

"Should I wake Roger up in California and pre-empt him finding this out from someone else?"

"Probably a good idea. You could take the approach that you are letting them know that their security has failed and you are requesting that they do something about it. Make it clear from the start that you do not believe any of this is your fault. Assume they are the negligent ones. Try to sound furious rather than apologetic."

"Okay."

"Did he have any idea how intimate you and Jo-Jo had become?"

"He knew we were getting on well. He saw her hug me the first night at his house. That was when he first suggested bringing you out to California. I don't know what else he knew."

"I would imagine he gets to find out pretty much everything that happens in that house."

"You think he has the rooms bugged?" The internal storm in my guts was growing worse by the minute.

"I'm sure there are a lot of security devices, not to mention all the phones and computers lying around everywhere with cameras and recording devices in them."

"Have you maybe been reading too many conspiracy theories? Too much science fiction perhaps?"

"You're the one whose guilty secrets are going viral. You are the one being paid a suspiciously large amount of money to write a Hollywood autobiography. You are the one who nearly got his head blown off in a school playground. You tell me how many conspiracies you think are going on in the world at any given moment."

It was my turn to fall silent as I tried to take everything in and work out the best way to limit the damage.

"Do you think that was why he invited me out?" she asked as she too processed all the new information. "Do you think he was worried you and Jo-Jo were getting too close?"

"What, jealous, do you mean?" I thought about it. "It's possible. I guess when he saw how friendly you and Jo-Jo became it must have put his mind at rest a bit. He definitely likes to believe he has total control over her life. But I got the impression they were just really good friends. That's what everyone told me. If he has a thing for her he certainly doesn't know how to vocalise it."

"Maybe he didn't like the idea of having to compete for the honour of being her bff."

"He did act kind of weird on the walk he took me on in the mountains. Oh God," more horror flooded my adrenaline system, "I wrote all about that in the diary too, and about meeting him in London and my first impressions of him. Those thoughts must all be out there now too."

"Publish and be damned eh?" she smiled, a little mirthlessly I thought. "Go talk to Roger. I'm okay, really."

I hugged her tight, more grateful than I could ever express for her kindness and understanding. She responded with what felt like all of her heart and all of her strength.

"Roger," I said when he picked up, sounding sleepy, "we have a leak. I need help from your tech people to plug it. The system they fitted wasn't fool proof. Someone has hacked into it and we need to talk about damage limitation."

"Okay," he was suddenly more awake. "Let me get online and work out what is happening."

It didn't take long for Jo-Jo's support network to start responding to the story. Nearly all the statements were accompanied by the iconic pictures of her and the children at the funeral.

"I needed a shoulder to cry on, really badly," one of her people wrote.

"Ghostwriters are good listeners, they don't judge," wrote another. "Writing a book with someone is an intimate experience. You inevitably get close."

I liked to think that she had originated these thoughts and they hadn't been dreamed up by Roger and his damage-limitation team but I knew that was unlikely. It was quite possible that the whole thing had been kept away from her, that she was still blissfully asleep. A different part of me hoped that was the case. I felt like I had betrayed her trust and her friendship by recording those private moments, when she had been at her most vulnerable and she had wanted me to be an "actual shoulder to cry on". But then did celebrities of her magnitude even expect to have private moments anymore?

* * *

The technicians who had installed the new computer were back at the house a few hours later, genuinely puzzled as to how anyone had been able to get through the security they had set up, their professional pride dented but their curiosity piqued at the same time. I tried asking them questions but they pretended to be concentrating too hard on whatever it was they were doing on my keyboard, which they had synchronised to their own keyboards, to hear me. I got the impression that both of them were more comfortable talking to machines than to real people.

By the time they had finished they assured me that I was as safe as I could be, but suggested that I continue writing my actual manuscripts on a machine that was not connected to the internet in any way. What I should have done, or so Caroline kept telling me, was switch off every other machine that day and just concentrated on the writing, but following a developing story on social media, especially when you are directly involved, is as tempting as chocolate and as addictive as heroin. I would write a few pages and then "take a break" so that I could check the hashtags and see what people were saying now.

There were so many threads to follow that I could have spent every hour of every day for the rest of my life on their track. There were all the conspiracy theories around Chuck's murder to start with. Was the killer a hired assassin? If so, who had hired him and what were their motives? If he was acting alone, what were his real motives? Were they what he claimed on the video, or was that a smokescreen to hide something even more sinister? Was Chuck his target from the start and the kids no more than "collateral damage"?

* * *

The story about Jo-Jo climbing into my bed for comfort had also taken on a life of its own, triggering a thousand different speculations. Was I lying? Was I making the whole story up to get my own fifteen minutes of fame? Had I actually had sex with her and was I lying about that aspect? Was I a great friend in a moment of need or a heartless cad taking advantage of a woman at a vulnerable moment? Was I a good friend or a terrible husband? The more literate members of the online community drew parallels with a scene in the Robert Harris book, *The Ghost*, between the ghostwriter and the wife of the ex-prime minister whose autobiography he is writing. Then there were those who wanted to know how Caroline felt about the whole thing. Was it okay for a married man to comfort a female friend in this way? Did she believe me when I said nothing happened? Would any intelligent woman trust their man in bed with Jo-Jo Win? Was I a sad "love-rat" for writing about the incident at all? One of my detractors decided that I must be a "total slimeball", which gave me considerable pause for thought and threw me off my writing stride for a whole precious hour. Another suggested I had deliberately leaked the diary material myself as a publicity stunt for the book or to boost my own ego. Others speculated, with an extraordinary confidence in the accuracy of their own imaginings, as to whether there was some far more sinister plot being hatched in the background by big business interests and, if so, they wondered what Roger Rex's role in the whole spider's web might be.

There was even one conspiracy theorist who managed to link Chuck's assassination with those of the Kennedy brothers and Martin Luther King. They didn't suggest it was the same assassin (who would presumably be too old or too dead to actually pull a trigger any more), but were convinced it was the same underlying forces at work, although they couldn't quite decide how much of it could be pinned on the Mafia and how much on the FBI.

* * *

I wanted to apologise to Jo-Jo for giving away something so personal without permission but I had no way of directly contacting her. I went through my phone looking for the messages she had sent me when I was staying at her house. I tried responding to the number they came from, but the calls met a blank wall. I didn't even know if she was aware that it was going on, or cared. She had never showed any interest in anything that was being said about her in any of the media while I was with her. I guess when you are being written and talked about all the time all over the world you have to cut yourself off from most of it because there wouldn't be enough hours in the day for a normal life otherwise (the time I was wasting on following these stories was evidence enough of that), plus all the misinformation would drive you insane. But maybe Roger would have shared this particular story with her since it would have an effect on her precious "platform" and would also impact the reception the book received when it came out.

It was like I was living my life in two different dimensions. In the cloud I was famous, or infamous, an object of envy and speculation to millions and an object of mockery to millions more. Yet as soon as I looked away from the screens my life was entirely unchanged. Maddy was still laughing happily around the house, the postman and milkman came and went as they always did and every now and then the phone would ring in the traditional old-fashioned way, usually with another mother wanting to gossip with Caroline about matters in the real world, like play dates and immunisations.

Caroline, as the wife in the "triangle", decided that she

would put out one statement to the online community and then would simply ignore the whole business. The statement was short and to the point.

"I believe my husband's story and am proud that he is the sort of man who a friend feels they can turn to for comfort at a time of trauma. I am well aware that he might find Jo-Jo Win attractive, since half the men in the world feel the same way, and quite a lot of the women. I too have been lucky enough to spend time with her, however, and feel confident that she is not the sort of woman who would steal another woman's husband."

I thought it was a great statement and watched in horror as the online community fell upon it like a pack of wolves, tearing it apart, reading a million different meanings into what looked to me like pretty straightforward words, some accusing her of being a naïve fool, others deciding she was a calculating schemer. Caroline saw none of these reactions, having very wisely gone back to concentrating on the books she was working on, clearing her desk in preparation for me handing over Jo-Jo's manuscript for her editorial attention.

"Any chance you can bring forward the delivery date for the final draft?" Roger asked after I had been writing solidly for a month. "Then we can take advantage of this wave of interest in Jo-Jo."

"Roger has asked me to finish the book a month early," I told Caroline when we next bumped into each other in the kitchen.

"In that case," she said, "you had better get off the internet and do some proper work."

"Fair point," I said, and went back to my office to switch the outside world off for a while.

23

☙❦

When I managed to concentrate, the book worked like a dream. It practically wrote itself. That happens sometimes, although not often. There is just so much material, so much to say, so many strong characters, so many questions to be answered for the readers, that once you start writing it just rolls forward on oiled wheels. I had completed it within another three weeks. I sent it to Roger. He had read it within hours and rang.

"It's so great!" he said. "You have absolutely nailed it. The message is perfect. I just wanted to keep turning the pages to find out what happened next and I already know the story. It's fantastic. I love the cover mock-ups Caroline has been sending through. This is all great. What do we do next?"

I could hardly believe that it was going to be this easy. I'd had books that went well before, but never anything as smooth as this.

"Have you shown it to Jo-Jo?" I asked.

"She'll love it," he said, "she trusts you completely."

That was also a relief to hear, since I had been waking up at night in a cold sweat ever since the leak, imagining how she must have felt about me describing our relationship the way I had, but I didn't like the idea of us charging ahead without even asking her. I would have preferred to hear that she was happy with it from her own mouth. It was more than possible that Roger was saying what he knew I wanted to hear.

"Shouldn't we wait until she has at least read it," I suggested, "in case there are any factual inaccuracies?"

"Sure, sure, we'll get everyone in the family to read it, but we need to be moving forward at the same time, so how do we do that?"

"The next stage would be to hire an editor. Caroline will take care of that."

"Okay. Tell her to get cracking. This is so great! I am really excited!"

* * *

I had seen a lot of missed calls from Giles on my phone and I had been putting off ringing back. I was pretty sure that he would have heard on the publishing grapevine that Caroline was handling all the design and editing side of the book and that Roger was intending to take care of the marketing and distribution himself. I imagined it was going to be an awkward conversation either way. He must have guessed I was ignoring his calls and used someone else's phone, catching me at a moment when I was in the garden with Maddy and distracted enough to answer a call from an unknown number.

He got straight to the point. "I know you must be really busy but I would really like to talk to both of you."

"You want to talk to Jo-Jo?"

"No. You and Caroline."

"We are a bit stretched at the moment ..."

"Why don't I take you both to dinner at Le Manoir?"

"That's a long way to drive for dinner, and we would have to find a babysitter ..." I probably wasn't sounding very convinced by my own excuses. Le Manoir was famous for being hard to get into and I knew that Caroline would like the idea of going there, but not the logistics.

"Why don't I book you a room there for the night, so you can make it a mini-break? My treat totally."

"We have a small child, Giles ..."

"Is there someone she could stay with for the night? It would be a nice break for both of you at a stressful time ..."

"Let me talk to Caroline."

"That's a tempting offer," Caroline said when I told her. "What does he want to talk about?"

"Maybe he wants to buy you out."

"You think?"

"I have no idea. A night at Le Manoir is going to cost

him as much as he paid you in a month when you worked for him, so I guess he must have a good reason."

* * *

The temptation proved too much. Maddy was set up to spend the night with her best friend – a prospect which seemed to fill her with a shockingly mature sense of joyous anticipation and none of the anxieties that we might have hoped she would feel at being separated for a whole night from both her parents. We were aware that we were over-protective, but that didn't mean we liked being reminded of our own dispensability.

"We should be grateful she is such a well-balanced indi-vidual already," Caroline said, rather doubtfully, as we drove away from dropping her, both of us feeling uncom-fortably incomplete.

The suite we had been given at Le Manoir was as luscious as the hotel's reputation had promised and Caroline sank herself into a hot bath before dinner, as if hoping to wash away the stress of years, in preparation for a dinner to match the luxury of the surroundings. Giles arrived with a woman called Marilyn, an American wearing a black beret at a rakish angle, who seemed to be in charge of global marketing for the whole group. It seemed that Giles was having pres-sure applied to him by the company's international board. It wasn't until near the end of the meal that I realised she must be the "old school friend" Roger had called for advice.

When small talk about the wonderfulness of the hotel and the food had been exhausted, and Caroline and I had said all we wanted to say – and as much as Giles and Marilyn could manage to show an interest in – about Maddy, and Giles had spent some time making a big deal about choosing the right wines, he finally got to the point.

"We understand just how much the ground is moving under the traditional publishing business model at the moment," he said, "and we completely understand that this is the right time for small, independent operations like yours to play a bigger role in the industry, but there is still a place for the old dinosaurs like us when it comes to handling the big stories. We would really like to find a way of working together."

"We would be more than happy to launch the book simultaneously into every international market," Marilyn added. "That is something you need a lot of global muscle to pull off successfully."

I refrained from pointing out that Roger Rex's empire had about a hundred times the "global muscle" of even one of the biggest international publishing groups.

The conversation meandered on for a while, punctuated by exclamations of wonder as each new course was served, and I assumed that we were just talking about Jo-Jo's book, but then Marilyn threw a small grenade into the conversation.

"So what are your plans for the diary?" she asked.

"Plans?" I was taken aback.

"When are you planning to publish that?"

"I have no plans," I said, glancing across at Caroline who seemed to be paying an unlikely amount of attention to the food on her plate.

"We think that Jo-Jo Win's autobiography is going to be huge," Giles took over again. "Which is why I have been trying to persuade you to work with us, obviously. But we also think your diary could be huge too, particularly given all this attention it has been getting ..."

"But I am tied hand and foot with confidentiality agreements," I protested. "I was just writing things down so that I didn't forget them and thinking that maybe at some time in the future I might be able to do something with them. I never expected anyone else to read them for years, if ever. Roger Rex has some ferocious lawyers."

"So do we," Giles said smoothly, "and it is the opinion of our ferocious lawyers that now the information is out in the public domain, thanks to your friendly hacker, through no fault of yours, it may well not be covered by those agreements any more."

"There is no way we want to spend the next ten years in court fighting Roger's lawyers over legal technicalities," I interrupted, "even if we do end up winning. Life is way too short for that."

"But you have a good relationship with him," Giles protested. "He trusts you, and so do Jo-Jo Win and her family."

"All the more reason not to go publishing stuff about

them that they would rather not have published," I pointed out.

"Of course," Giles paused while one waiter refilled his glass and another asked us for the twentieth time if everything was to our satisfaction, "but you don't have to go behind their backs. Roger Rex's big thing is transparency, right?"

"It's certainly one of his big things," I agreed.

"Well, allowing you to publish your personal account of the whole thing would fit nicely into that philosophy, showing they have nothing to hide, that everything is above board and so on."

"Can I just check," Caroline spoke up, having been listening in silence for some time. "This is just the autobiography of a film star we are discussing here, right?"

"No," Giles paused, as if choosing his words really carefully and we then had to wait while yet another waiter came to talk about dessert wines. Eventually he was able to continue. "I don't think that is all we are talking about here. Why would someone as busy and as rich as Roger Rex be putting this much time and thought into the project if that was all it was. There is something much bigger in play here and that is why I think you might benefit from having us as part of your team."

24

ℬℭ

Our time was so completely taken up with the editing and designing of Jo-Jo's book over the next few weeks that Caroline and I didn't have a moment to really talk any further about Giles's offer of help.

"This cover is great!" Roger enthused once it was finalised. The main image, predictably, was one of the pictures of Jo-Jo and the kids at the funeral. Roger had insisted on it and the designer had made it look incredibly moody. "This is fantastic. Great characterisation, great pictures! It brings the whole family alive. I love everything about it."

So much did he love it that he told us he planned to order an initial print-run of several hundred thousand copies, although he remained unusually reluctant to let us know the exact figure. His marketing department did a remarkable job on making the book available in supermarkets the world over, and beside the tills in random retail outlets like petrol stations and local grocery stores that previously had only ever offered blockbuster movies and video games (many of which, of course, starred a Lycra-clad Jo-Jo). His social media battalions ensured that the internet buzzed with extracts and reviews and comments, both good and bad. I started out being sensitive to every negative comment but soon became so overwhelmed by the sheer quantity of opinions being generated that I had to switch the internet off again.

I had also had to stop answering my phone because the traditional media had now picked the story up from the internet and all wanted to do interviews and profiles. Roger had insisted that my name should be clearly visible on the cover of the book as well as the title page, completely over-ruling everything that had been specified about my anonymity in the original contract I had signed. When I tried to talk him out of it, panic-stricken at the thought of so much exposure, he told me that it was Jo-Jo who was insisting, not wanting people to accuse her of trying to pass the book off as all her own work. I didn't feel I could refuse Jo-Jo anything, as Roger no doubt guessed.

Not only was I nervous that if I did interviews I would say something that would rattle the cages of the lawyers, I was also unwilling to be endlessly grilled about any personal feelings I might have for Jo-Jo, either as a friend, a client or a film-star crush. Also, there were not enough hours in the day to deal with all the enquiries and to live a normal family life, and I certainly didn't want to start hiring my own public relations team. So I simply switched everything off and pretended none of it was happening, while being aware all the time of a tiny knot of excitement in the pit of my stomach at the thought of how many people were now reading my words in the full knowledge that they had been written by me.

By temporarily cutting ourselves off from any potentially interactive media, we were probably amongst the last people in the western world to hear that Jo-Jo had announced she was going to run as a democratic candidate in the next presidential race. We saw her picture on the television news while reading to Maddy and had to unmute it to hear what was being said. Neither of us spoke for several minutes, our mouths hanging open, so obviously stunned that Maddy also stared at the screen, following our gazes, as if trying to understand what it was that had had such a dramatic effect on both her parents.

"Is that what the whole thing has been about from the beginning, then?" Caroline asked.

"I think it might be. Right from the beginning everyone was saying the book should be like Obama's *Dreams from my Father*. That would certainly explain why Roger has been spending so much time and money on building her platform."

"To put his friend and protégé in the White House?"

"Absolutely."

"Why wouldn't he put himself forward if he wants the White House?"

"A large proportion of the world hates the wealthy 'one

per cent' at the moment," I said, thinking it all through as I talked. It was like a mist was clearing before my eyes and things were starting to come into focus that I now realised should have been obvious to me all the time. "Plus Roger has trouble with making eye contact or keeping to any one subject for more than twenty seconds. No one would vote for him to run the country, right? But we know the public likes voting actors and celebrities into positions of power, as long as they have the right back stories and as long as people trust and believe what they say."

"So that was your job, to provide the back story necessary to win over the electorate?"

"Looks like it."

"Sucker!" she laughed, lifting Maddy up and snuggling close to me. "Seriously, though. Good job done." She held up her palm and I obliged with a high five. "So maybe now we should think about publishing the diary? Or at least taking legal advice on whether we can."

It was hard to believe how totally our lives had changed within a few months. The money had come through exactly as promised and we had been able to pay off our mortgage and start a savings account for Maddy. Even once we had put aside what we estimated would be necessary to meet whatever tax bills might arrive, we still had enough to support ourselves for a year or two. It was like a giant weight had been lifted from our shoulders. There seemed no need to take any immediate decisions on what to do with the diary material. I had mentioned the idea of publishing it in passing to Roger a couple of weeks earlier.

"Great. Great. That sounds very exciting," he said, but I could tell he wasn't totally concentrating on what I was saying. When I told Caroline his reaction we decided to wait and see what happened next. It didn't seem necessary to cash in on the huge publicity the leak had created. People working in the publishing business were not going to forget this story in a long time. We could afford to stay aloof for a bit, maintaining what seemed to us like a dignified silence.

With time on our hands now that the book was published, we also found ourselves taking a keen interest in the mainstream news cycle for the first time ever, as the American election machine slowly ground into action.

To start with many people dismissed Jo-Jo as a joke candidate, the beautiful film star looking for ways to raise her profile. But as people began to hear her talk about the things that were important to her, the impression changed. Instead of a film star they saw a brave young widow of mixed race, someone whose ancestors had come to America with nothing and had done great work. There was a fair amount of gossip about Lillian's past, but the majority of the nation now applauded a woman who had seemed to be a victim but had turned her situation around and made something good of her life. There were several zeitgeists working in Jo-Jo's favour. The first was that she was a woman and a large portion of the American public was ready to have another try at voting in their first female president. The second was that she was offering a reaction to the authoritarianism of the last few years and a return to the sort of liberal values that had been gaining traction over the previous century.

There were also plenty of people vehemently against everything she stood for, of course; people who didn't like the concept of women in power, didn't like her mixed-race background, didn't think she had the experience, didn't like the idea of a celebrity running for power and didn't like her opinions on gun control. But all these naysayers found it hard to win against her in debates on any of those platforms because she was entirely open and unashamed about all of them. Whenever the subject of Lillian's past came up she was able to point people to the book. When people claimed she wasn't really American because she spent so much of her childhood living in the developing world, she could point them to her father's humanitarian achievements, all of which we had talked about in the book.

Her one Achilles heel seemed to be that she was so obviously a senior member of the "global liberal elite", a label which allowed her opponents to dismiss her as being "out of touch" and accuse her of patronising ordinary people. Rivals kept talking about her friendship with Roger Rex and his influence on her from behind the scenes, and wild figures were bandied about regarding how much all her investments in high-tech start-ups might now be worth. There were some rumours circulating that she had invested heavily in crypto-currencies when they first came out and that her holdings were now worth many billions. If that was so, it was the first I had heard of it.

Deep in the world's subconscious, however, were lodged images from her enormously popular early films, in which she played the tough girl from the wrong side of the tracks, seeking retribution with her guns and her fists, obviously sexy despite her androgynous outfits. The subliminal message was that she might be part of the liberal elite now, but she came from a kick-ass background and so understood exactly how tough you have to be to survive on the streets in the twenty-first century. This element of her history also helped soften her message about gun control. She was able to speak against guns both from the perspective of someone who had lost her husband and almost lost her children to a gunman, and from the perspective of someone who was perfectly capable of using weapons herself if the situation required. It was hard for her rivals to dismiss her as a "snowflake" when there was an image of her firmly lodged in people's minds as a violent vigilante.

Some people tried to attack her mothering skills, accusing her of choosing her career over her children. The general public, however, had got to know and like Martin and Lillian in the television show, and most were perfectly happy to think that Harvey and Bette were in their grand-parents' safe hands whenever their mother was away campaigning.

Her rivals for the democratic nomination started to fall by the wayside. Most of those who stepped aside then sensed a bandwagon getting under way and announced that they were going to be backing her candidacy. Within a few months of the initial announcement the idea that she was a credible candidate had taken root. Several hundred thousand more copies of the book were printed and distributed. Her eloquence and the authority which she had over the big crowds that turned out to listen to her were surprising. People began to talk about her as a serious candidate and sales of the book continued to rise. Journalists all over the world quoted passages from it as if they were directly quoting Jo-Jo herself.

"Maybe you should have negotiated yourself a piece of the action here," Caroline teased when the book became simultaneously lodged at number one in both the *New York Times* and the *Sunday Times* bestseller lists for several weeks.

"Maybe," I agreed, feeling a tiny seed of doubt taking root in my stomach. Had I been rash in not taking an agent or lawyer to that meeting at the beginning? "But I very much like the feeling of having money safely stowed away in the bank."

She laughed and kissed me fondly. "You're not going to find me arguing with that."

25

૭૦૭

On the night of the election we did not go to bed. I'm not going to say that we didn't doze off now and then, entwined on the sofa, but we were fully awake when the results began to look conclusive. America was going to have their first female president and it was going to be someone with impeccable liberal credentials. Maybe it was because we had not had a decent night's sleep, but neither of us was fully able to take the news in. To become, within eighteen months, someone who knew and was involved with the people now taking over the most powerful position in the world, did not seem real.

We watched Jo-Jo coming out to take the applause of her supporters, followed by Harvey and Bette, both looking much more grown-up than we remembered, and also much more vulnerable. Balloons fell from the ceiling, snow storms of confetti swirled around them and victorious people cheered and wept and leapt in the air with joy.

Some pundits were coming forward to predict that this was a final take-over of the world by Silicon Valley, claiming that the dinosaurs of the industrial eras had finally been removed and the new world order was safely in place. Others were saying it was yet more evidence that the worlds of politics and entertainment had become inextricably enmeshed forever. The western world's population, they said, now believed that the superficial values of extreme beauty, extreme wealth and extreme celebrity were worthy replacements for gravitas, intellectual achievement and political experience. Those who celebrated the loudest, however, were those who believed that the transparency of celebrity life and reality television would now come even further into the White House and the people would be able to gain an even deeper, and more accurate, understanding of those who they had elected to govern them.

* * *

We heard very little from Roger during those campaigning months, and not at all from Jo-Jo. It was not a surprise, first because they must have been busy on a scale that most mortals could hardly even comprehend, and second because that is how relationships between ghostwriters and their clients often go. During the months of interviewing and editing you become intimate in a way that normally only happens between clients and medical professionals like therapists or psychoanalysts. Once the book is completed the bond is immediately severed, unless there is a follow-up project being planned. I was not, therefore, surprised not to have heard from anyone in the presidential circle, and I was taken completely unawares when I received an email from Roger, marked "strictly confidential". It bore all his trademarks of brevity.

We are planning to get married in a private ceremony at the house. We would love you and Caroline to come. Bring Maddy too. Julia will be in contact with details. Please don't mention this to anyone. Roger.

I had to read it several times before I could be sure that I hadn't misunderstood. I took it to show Caroline.

"Do we assume 'we' means him and Jo-Jo?" she asked.

"I guess so."

"The President of the United States is going to marry one of the world's richest men? That all seems very Jackie O."

"Not to mention '*House of Cards*'," I added.

"Quite," we fell silent for a few moments.

"Why would Jo-Jo want to marry Roger?" I asked.

"Why did Jackie Kennedy want to marry Onassis? Why did Diana want to marry Charles? Why did Melania ..."

"Okay," I said. "I get it. But she's the President and she has all the money she could possibly need."

"Probably feels like a pretty lonely place to be," she suggested. "And anyway, she won't be there forever. Every mother needs security for her children. But maybe we're being unfair, maybe she loves the guy. But how come we get to be on the guest list? Don't they have a million friends and family they want to ask?"

"Who knows how many other people will be there," I said, "I mean, you could fit a lot of people onto that estate. I know. I've walked over most of it"

26

ෂා৩

Julia was just as efficient as I remembered her, except now she appeared to have real power, and a two piece suit and an expensive, glossy haircut to prove it. Not only were our flights arranged, an official driver from the American embassy arrived to take us right to the door of the plane. The same happened at the other end – Julia now being way too busy with secret wedding plans to be able to spare the time to do airport pick-ups in person. Everyone involved in getting us from our front door to Roger's was immensely polite and efficient and utterly unwilling to engage in any sort of personal conversation that might risk giving away any sort of information about anything. They were all entirely attentive to our needs, without ever quite engaging with us in anything approaching a personal conversation. Some of them, of course, were listening to voices in their ear-pieces; others were constantly scanning surrounding buildings, presumably for the tell-tale glint of a sniper's rifle or paparazzo's camera.

Jo-Jo had not yet arrived from Washington and the house was fully under Julia's control. She took a few seconds to welcome us but was almost immediately distracted by her phone and gestured for us to make ourselves at home, signalling that she would catch up with us later and managing to make it seem like she not only meant it but was actually looking forward to the prospect.

The children, along with their newly acquired nanny, had already been flown in. The room where I had been questioned by the FBI agents had been designated a "family room" and equipped with the sort of things Roger obviously imagined children liked to play with, making it look a little like an Apple showroom. Both of them were curled up on one of the sofas, drawing pictures and being discreetly photographed by the same woman who had enshrined their images so effectively at their father's funeral. Both children greeted us enthusiastically. It was a relief to find someone who was willing to communicate with us as real people. Maddy immediately seemed to remember Bette and happily climbed out of my arms in order to be embraced by someone far more interesting.

"What are you drawing?" I asked, joining them on the sofa.

"It's Mommy," Bette said, holding it up for me to see how far her artistic abilities had progressed since we first met. "She's the Queen of America now."

"She's not a queen, stupid," her brother corrected her. "She's Madam President. If she met your English Queen," he turned to me, "who would be the most powerful?"

"Hmm, good question," I admitted. "Well, your mummy would definitely be the most powerful at the moment, but the Queen keeps her power for much longer." I could almost hear the cogs turning in their brains as they both continued to concentrate on their pictures, having furnished Maddy with paper and a crayon of her own.

"So," Harvey came back after a few seconds, "if a baddie was going to blow up the world and all the kings and queens and presidents in the world had to work together to defeat him ..."

"Like superheroes?" I asked.

"Yeah. Would Mommy be the boss of them?"

Bette looked at me and raised her eyes in despair at her brother's childish obsessions.

"Yeah, I guess she would be the boss," I said, "what's your picture of?"

"It's Daddy," he said, turning it for me to see. Chuck had become a sort of flying cowboy, guns blazing in each hand and blond hair flying behind him. "He's coming to rescue us," he explained.

"You and Bette?" I asked.

"And Mommy."

"Wow, that's great. I like the way he's got bare feet."

"He has karate superpowers. He can kick anyone to death if he has to."

"So," Caroline interrupted quickly, probably suspecting that I was about to ask one question too many and cause the boy a lifetime of psychological problems. "Are you looking forward to the wedding this afternoon?"

"I've had a dress specially made," Bette announced, "and Mommy's hairdresser is going to do my hair with flowers, and I've got a bouquet like Mommy's."

"You are going to be a proper princess," I said.

"Can we put flowers in Maddy's hair too?"

"I don't see why not," Caroline said. "What about you Harvey? What are you going to be wearing?"

Harvey made a face. "A stupid suit, like weird Roger."

Bette had obviously heard but said nothing, keeping her eyes on her picture.

"Do you think Roger's weird?" I laughed, unable to resist probing further, avoiding Caroline's warning looks.

"Soooo weird," he said. "He doesn't even like going to the beach. He never even goes in his own swimming pool – which is painted black! How weird is that?"

"Mommy says he is one of the cleverest men in the world," Bette kept drawing as she talked, "and she says we will be able to learn a lot from him if we want to."

"Who wants to learn to be weird?" her brother sneered.

"You're weird," Bette muttered.

"I wouldn't mind a swim now," I admitted. "Anyone fancy a quick dip in the black pool?"

"Harvey thinks there are monsters living at the bottom," his sister taunted.

"Then I shall fight them," I said, standing up and striking a defiant pose, "and emerge victorious! Who's with me?"

Caroline and Bette declined the invitation, wanting to spend time planning Maddy's wedding outfit. As Harvey and I made our way up to the swimming pool I was aware that every inch of our route was monitored by discreet eyes and reported into discreet microphones. Once we were in the water, battling and splashing loudly against the monsters that lurked in the deep end, I noticed men in dark glasses moving about on the other terraces, watching the sky and the horizon, tasked with keeping us safe from all harm. A small cloud of smoke gave away the photographer as she watched and clicked from the shadows of the surrounding palm trees in their angular pots, shots that I guessed would one day appear in coffee table books about the era we were now living through. I wondered if there was any chance that the rest of Harvey's life could be anything but an anti-climax after a start like this. Or would he continue to have huge things happening to him all his life, and if so, would he survive them and live long enough to be able to reflect back with any sort of nostalgic affection?

When Lillian and Martin arrived, Lillian took over from the nanny and summoned Harvey from the pool, wrapping him in a large grey towel and sweeping him away to be prepared for the ceremony. Part of me was relieved. It was hard work waging wars on monsters without the support of Chuck's enthusiasm for the battle. I found Martin in the kitchen making a coffee.

"Hey," he looked genuinely pleased to see me, "good to see you again. Can I get you a coffee? Black, no sugar, right?"

We found ourselves a quiet corner to sit.

"Been meaning to get in touch," he said, "ever since reading the book. Good job. Well done. I even spotted Lillian dabbing away a tear."

"Thanks."

"Made me sound a little like Julie Andrews in *The Nun's Story*, but good job none the less."

"Audrey Hepburn."

"What?"

"*The Nun's Story*. It was Audrey Hepburn, not Julie Andrews."

"Oh," he laughed. "Julie Andrews was a nun too though, right?"

"Maria in *The Sound of Music*. And she was *Mary Poppins*, so the reference works. She's done well then, your little girl."

"So it seems." He sipped his coffee. "All the Tiger Mother's dreams have paid off. Poor old Chuck. I miss him."

"He was a good guy," I agreed. "Not sure whether he would have liked the restrictions of being a White House husband though. Not much surfing to be had in Washington."

"He'd have enjoyed Camp David."

There were so many questions I wanted to ask. He was staring me straight in the eye, a slight smile on his lips, as if daring me to delve a bit further, entertained by my caution. A secret service man hovered, just out of earshot, but I was pretty sure there wouldn't be any conversations going on anywhere in this house that weren't being recorded for posterity one way or another.

"She'll make a great president," I said instead.

"Lillian?"

"Well, that wasn't who I was thinking of, but I'm sure she would be a great president too."

"You betcha!" He seemed genuinely amused by the thought.

"I meant Jo-Jo."

"Yeah, she'll be a great president. She got my vote," he laughed again.

"Does she love him, do you think?" I asked.

He didn't answer for a second before responding with another question. "Do you think she's going to have much time for love and romance over the next few years? This is a pretty grown up job she's taken on here."

"I suppose he has the resources to make her life easier in a lot of ways," I suggested. Martin didn't respond. "What about your grandchildren. How are they doing?"

"They're tough. They've got plenty of support. They've got Lillian on their team too; how could they possibly fail to thrive? They wouldn't dare."

We saw Roger's helicopter coming in through the mountains and half an hour later there was a sound of bustle outside the room and the roar of powerful engines, suggesting that the presidential motorcade had arrived.

"I think this may be our cue to go get ready for the ceremony," Martin said. "See you in church."

27

ഇ൪

A canopy had been erected on one of the terraces and there were so many flowers; it was a minute or two before I realised how few guests were there. It was like the scene in the DiCaprio version of *Gatsby*, where he fills the cottage with flowers in order to impress Daisy or, as the narrator puts it in the book, "a greenhouse arrived from Gatsby's, with numerous receptacles to contain it".

The secret service men had made themselves invisible behind the pillars of white roses. Because Maddy had been recruited into the bridal party, Caroline was with her and I went to find a seat on my own. A choir was singing, very beautifully, which covered up the deathly silence that would otherwise have occurred. A distinguished looking African-American bishop was sitting quietly at the front, pretending to read the prayer book open on his lap. There was none of that subdued, excited chatter and laughter that usually precede the arrival of a bride as relatives and friends reunite and recognise one another, sometimes for the first time in many years. There weren't many seats to choose from, so there obviously weren't many more guests expected, and Julia pointed me to one in the second row. She suggested I keep the one on the aisle free for Caroline when she came in.

On my other side was a white haired man who I had seen walking towards the terrace earlier. I had noticed him partly because of the exceptionally good cut of his blue suit and partly because of his heavy reliance on an ebony cane to keep himself upright, and his extreme frailty.

"Hi," I said, extending my hand. "Andrew."

"Gianni," the old man replied, shaking my hand with long, shockingly bony fingers.

"Oh, hi!" I said, realising who he was for the first time.

"Have we met?" he asked, a puzzled look crossing his once handsome, now deeply lined face.

"No, but I recently wrote a book with Jo-Jo and she talked about you."

"Ah, you are the writer. She sent me a copy with a letter inside. She told me that you had become good friends. I read the book. You said some kind things about our time together."

"Only things that she had said to me first. I think you had a big impact on her, particularly on her creative side."

"Yes, so I read. She had a big impact on me too. She's the only person I have met who I think I can truly say has a musical soul. It was very gratifying to read that she enjoyed our time together too. She has always been an exceptional woman. Well, I don't have to tell you that. You must have spent a lot of time together in order to catch her voice so clearly. I will be honest with you, Andrew, you may be surprised to hear it, looking at me now, but I broke a lot of hearts in my youth. But she broke mine more completely than anyone else ever could. Can you imagine what a burden it is to have your heart broken by a woman whose face is then going to become one of the most visible in the world? It was a terrible time."

"But you have stayed friends, despite everything?"

"She reached out to me when she became president and decided to marry. That was when she sent the book. I had not heard from her for many, many years."

"But you accepted the invitation for today?"

"If you have someone that fascinating in your life, you would have to be very foolish to shut them out completely, however painful it might be to see them, don't you think? Obviously you do because you are here when there is no professional need because the book is all written and published. Do you attend the weddings of many of your clients?"

"No," I laughed. "Not many. Not many people seem to have been invited today, do they?"

"Isn't it nice to know that we are amongst the few people she wanted here today?"

"Yes," I agreed, "I suppose it is."

"We have been anointed by the Gods," he smiled wistfully, his eyes following Lillian, who had taken her seat in the front row and was studiously avoiding looking at both of us.

Roger's suit was obviously expensive and must have been made to measure, but it still gave the impression of not fitting very well as he came hurrying in to take his place at the front, ready to see his bride-to-be make her entrance. There didn't even seem to be a best man. Gianni turned his head slowly to face me and raised both eyebrows at once.

"Do you know Roger?" I whispered.

"Only from what I have read in the newspapers. I'm told he has a first class brain." I thought I saw a whisper of a smile on the old man's lips, but at that moment Roger jumped to his feet and we knew that we should follow suit. Gianni wobbled a little and I steadied his elbow as we rose together and turned to look.

Jo-Jo looked like an angel, one arm resting on her father's sleeve as she came down the short aisle with the children walking in front of her. Maddy looked inordinately pleased with herself, proudly keeping her head up so that she did not dislodge the carefully placed flowers. Harvey and Bette both kept their eyes on the floor. Jo-Jo's dress skimmed above the ground and was a simple design, hugging the contours of her body at the top, the skirt moving softly with the breeze coming in from the mountains. Tiny diamonds glinted in her perfectly formed earlobes and around her neck, on a chain so slender it was invisible to my naked eyes. As she passed us I could smell the perfume on her skin and in her hair, like jasmine on a warm Mediterranean evening, and I heard Gianni taking a deep breath beside me.

"America is a very lucky country," the old man whispered in my ear. His eyes were moist with tears.

Caroline slipped into her seat from behind a pillar as we sat down, ready to scoop Maddy up should her nerve fail her, but our child seemed perfectly happy to sit on a smaller seat between Bette and Harvey, her eyes glued in wonder to the transcendently lovely bride with a distant look in her eyes, the smiling bishop and the fidgeting groom.

The ceremony was moving because Jo-Jo and the children were so beautiful, the flowers so bountiful and the choir so celestial. Gianni appeared to enter some sort of dream-state throughout, his eyes distant and glistening with memories which could have been happy or sad for all I could say. Roger gave his vows in a voice which was just slightly too loud to be appropriate while Jo-Jo's voice was little more than a whisper.

Once the ceremony was over we remained, standing amongst the floral pillars, being served champagne and canapés. Gianni had seemed to have trouble rising from his seat, even with the help of the cane, but once he was balanced he leaned his full weight on my arm. Lillian was suddenly there, gripping his other arm. She wasn't smiling.

"Hello Lillian," he said, a slight smile showing at the

corners of his mouth, as if his presence there might be some sort of small victory.

"I did not see your name on the guest list," she said and I could see that Martin was watching us from across the room, poised to join the group if his diplomacy was needed.

"It was a special request from the President," Jo-Jo said from behind me. "It wasn't easy to find you Gianni."

She stepped past me and I breathed in the aroma of jasmine again as she put her arms around his neck, kissing him slowly with her lips on both his cheeks and looking directly into his eyes.

"I imagine the President can find anyone if she truly wants to," Gianni smiled and bowed. "I've missed you."

"I was very afraid you might be dead," Jo-Jo said and it seemed to me that this simple, brutal phrase meant something more to both of them than it did to the rest of us.

"Do you need transport, Gianni?" Lillian asked, ignoring her daughter's arrival in the group.

"My driver is waiting for me," he said, tearing his eyes away from Jo-Jo's and looking directly at me. "May I borrow your arm?"

"Of course," I said, waiting for a few more moments as Jo-Jo kissed him again, placing her fingers on his shoulder, the diamonds in her engagement ring glinting in the sun. It looked like a final farewell.

It was him who pulled away first, bowing politely to the group before beginning the long walk out through the house, leaning heavily on my arm. He didn't speak again until he was about to climb into his waiting car. He pressed an engraved calling card into my hand.

"I am going to be in London next week," he said. "I would very much like to buy you lunch. I think you would be interested to know more."

When I got back to the group Jo-Jo had been swallowed up by a group of Mexican relatives.

"It is just family now," Lillian informed me as I rejoined her and I caught Caroline's eye.

"Of course," I said. "We need to be on our way."

I took Caroline's hand and we went over to Jo-Jo, who could see we were coming to say goodbye.

"Thank you both so much for coming all this way," she said, hugging us.

"The pleasure is absolutely ours," I assured her. "We are honoured to be part of such a select group."

"I only invited people who are really special to me," she said, squeezing both our hands at the same time, "and you two have shown yourselves to be very true friends indeed. I want you to know how much I appreciate it."

I opened my mouth to say that I was pleased to have met Gianni.

"Jo-Jo, come and cut the cake," Lillian called out from across the room. Jo-Jo gave us a small smile and obeyed.

* * *

I texted the mobile number on the card that Gianni had given me as soon as we got back to England, saying how pleased I had been to meet him and his response was instant.

Would you be my guest for lunch at the RAC Club in Pall Mall tomorrow at noon?

I would be delighted, I replied. *I look forward to it.*

The following day I was shown to the lounge area of the club by one of the porters who manned the doors. Gianni was already sitting, reading a newspaper with a gin and tonic at his elbow. I was shocked to see that he looked even thinner than he had a few days before, his cheeks sunken even further in, his neck half the size of his perfectly ironed shirt collar and Hermes tie.

"I hope this will be all right for you," he gestured around the grand room, "my family have been members here for many years, so it is like a home from home for me. We were in the automobile business for many generations."

"It's perfect," I assured him, sinking into the sofa beside his armchair and taking up his suggestion of ordering myself a gin and tonic. I had a feeling it was going to be an interesting few hours and I felt completely comfortable with my host.

We talked superficially for a few minutes about our trips back to Europe, comparing the services of different airlines, as travellers tend to do. Once my drink had been brought to me he put his feather-light hand on mine and leaned close.

"I am going to talk very frankly to you today," he said. "As you have no doubt guessed, I am very sick. I will not live long, so I cannot waste time playing games and being discreet. I have nothing to fear any more from lawyers or assassins or anyone else. None of them can touch me now because the grim reaper will get to me first."

"I'm sorry to hear that."

He brushed my sympathy aside as if impatient that I was already wasting his precious remaining time. "It will be completely up to you whether or not you choose to share what I am going to tell you with anyone else, but I would like to know that someone has heard my side of the story before I am finally silenced, and I can see that you have Jo-Jo's best interests at heart, that you care about her. You will be the best judge of what to do with the story and when to do it."

I took a sip of the gin and nodded my willingness to hear what I supposed was going to be something like a deathbed confession.

"I should never have become involved with Jo-Jo. If I had met her today, in the current political climate, I doubt if I would have had the courage to become her lover. I was more than thirty five years older than her and I was in effect her teacher. I was only a visiting teacher, technically I had no responsibilities for her pastoral care – but still ..."

He let the image sink into my mind. I seemed to remember that Jo-Jo was seventeen or eighteen when she met him in London, so he would then have been in his early fifties. That was an age gap which would not have played well in the media of today. I had googled him while I was writing that section of the book and had found pictures of him from that period. He cut a dashing figure and it was not hard to see why a young girl would have been susceptible to his charms.

"I have not lived a saintly life," he admitted, as if reading my thoughts. "There were many women before her and some of them were many years younger than me. Beautiful women were my weakness and I had a great deal of good fortune over the years in persuading them to share my bed. Jo-Jo was different to any that I had met before. I dare say that will not surprise you."

"No," I smiled conspiratorially, foolish man to foolish man, "that does not surprise me."

"The fact that she was so beautiful was coincidental, as was her age. She seemed to me to be the oldest and wisest soul I had ever met. Even if she had not agreed to be my lover I would have wanted her to be my friend. I just wanted to be with her every moment of the day. People do not become global superstars for nothing, do they? They have to have some deeper quality than mere looks or an ability to act or sing. We all recognise the real stars when we meet them, don't we? Even the ones that choose not to become famous."

"Yes," I said, never having thought about it in quite those terms before, "I suppose we do."

"Anyway, Jo-Jo asked if she could come to one of my concerts at the Albert Hall, so I arranged it and then we went for dinner afterwards, with many other people, and she shone. I think everyone at the table was in love with her by the end of the meal, but it was me she chose to go home with, after which she simply stayed. It seemed completely obvious that we should be together. It was the most fantastic summer. We were inseparable. I had some engagements around Europe, some musical, others to do with family business that I could not get out of, so she travelled with me, giving up the course that she was supposed to be doing in London. There were a lot of angry phone calls from Lillian – I'm sure you can imagine."

"The Tiger Mother baring her claws."

"Indeed," he chuckled, which caused him to cough for an uncomfortable length of time, the bones of his shoulders showing through his jacket as he bent forward. Eventually he recovered his breath. "In the end Jo-Jo got me to talk directly to her father on the phone. We got on well. He was obviously worried about his daughter and I assured him that I was looking after her."

A waiter informed us that our table was ready and it took Gianni all of his energy to get out of the chair, even with my help, and shuffle the short distance through to the Great Gallery. I walked behind him, aware that he did not have enough breath to walk and talk at the same time, bracing myself to catch him should he stumble. The waiter took through our gin glasses. Gianni sank into the white, armed chair, which the waiter had pulled out for him, with a sigh of relief. We both studied the menus in silence while his breathing returned to normal, and then ordered. Gianni knew exactly what wine he wanted without looking at the list.

"So," he said, breaking into the bread he had selected from the proffered basket and digging at the butter with his knife, "where was I?"

"Reassuring Martin you would look after his daughter."

"Yes, indeed. Such a reasonable man. Such a good man. I mean he can't have liked the idea of his daughter going out with a man older than himself, but I think he knew Jo-Jo well enough to know that if she had made her mind up he would not be able to persuade her she was making a mistake."

The wine waiter reappeared to show Gianni the bottle, pouring him a mouthful to taste. Gianni showed approval with a slight nod, waiting while both our glasses were filled and we were alone again.

"I went with her to the airport when it came to the end of the holidays and she had to return to California. It was the worst day of my life, even though I was certain at that stage we were going to be together in the end. I had to tell myself that, otherwise I would not have been able to stand the pain of seeing her go. I would not have been physically capable of letting go. I knew she had to finish her education and that I was going to have to be strong and patient over the next few years."

"You were certain the relationship would work, even with such a big age gap?" I asked.

"I know that sounds deluded," he nodded ruefully, swirling the wine in his glass, "and perhaps there was a part of me that knew I was living in a dream, but another part of me knew that if I forced myself to wake up from that dream I would certainly die from a broken heart."

He took a mouthful of wine and masked another coughing fit as best he could with the heavy linen napkin. It took him a long time to be able to talk again.

"It was not so easy to keep in touch in those days, if you remember. We wrote letters," he reached into his jacket pocket and produced a thin bundle of envelopes, tied together, placing them on the table between us. "These are hers to me. I can't bring myself to destroy them and you are the only person I can think of to pass them on to."

"What do you want me to do with them?" I asked, resisting the powerful temptation to pick them up and start reading.

"I will leave that to your judgement. You could destroy them, or you could send them back to Jo-Jo."

"Why have you not returned them to her?"

"I would doubt she gets to open her own post," he raised an eyebrow, "wouldn't you?"

I tried to remember if I had seen Jo-Jo receiving any mail apart from papers given to her by her assistant. I couldn't quite picture it happening. "No, you're probably right. So what happened next?"

The waiter arrived with our starters, causing him to pause again.

"What happened next?" he said once the waiter had gone. "I received a visit. I was performing at the Teatro Massimo in Palermo, in Sicily. Do you know it?"

"No, I'm afraid not."

"Fabulous venue, wonderful acoustics. The performance had been a great success. When I returned to my hotel they were waiting in the room ..."

He took a mouthful of carpaccio and started chewing, as if there was no more to be said.

"Who was waiting?" I urged, once I was sure he did not intend to continue unprompted.

He looked at me and his eyes were becoming watery once more. He took another mouthful with great deliberation.

"You need to understand a little about my family," he said eventually. "We have been in business for a very long time. We are all connected; my brothers, my father, his brothers, my grandfather and my great grandfathers, the families that we all married into. We are all connected, interdependent. There are debts and favours owed; grudges and vendettas that go back more than a century. It is very, very complicated."

He returned his attention to his carpaccio and I stayed silent, letting him choose his own time to continue.

"You talked a little in your book about Lillian's past," he said, sitting back contentedly once his plate was clean.

"Before she met Martin, you mean?"

"Indeed."

"In Las Vegas?"

He looked at me and gave a thin smile, as if he didn't need to say any more because I should now have the complete picture.

"Your family has interests in Las Vegas?" I said, trying to remember everything that I had ever heard about the creation of Las Vegas by the Mafia. "That's who came to see you? She was able to reach out to a Las Vegas contact after so long?"

"I imagine," he said, once our plates had been removed, "that Lillian was capable of exerting the same power over men that her daughter would be able to twenty years later. I would have been willing to kill for Jo-Jo, had she asked me to, even twenty years after she flew away to America."

"They threatened to kill you?"

"Not really a threat," he said, taking another mouthful of wine as he tried to think of the right way to describe the scene. "More of a promise. They just made it clear that I would die, as would several other members of my family, all of whom I cared about a great deal, and that Jo-Jo's life would also be made a misery until she realised the error of her ways. It was not a threat because a threat you can choose to ignore. I was not given any choice in this matter. I was simply being informed that the relationship was being ended."

The waiter returned with our main courses and I picked up the love letters, keen to get them into my pocket before he changed his mind. Not wanting to appear too eager I made it look like I was merely making room for the plates.

He didn't protest, giving no indication that he had even noticed. He obviously had no further interest in them now that he was dying.

"Lillian felt so strongly about ending the relationship that she got the Mafia involved?" I said, slowly, trying to get everything straight in my head as I took my first mouthful of Dover sole.

"She wanted the best for her daughter, and the best was not a man who would soon be old and dying," he gestured towards his own frail body. "Now her son-in-law is one of the richest, cleverest men in the world and her daughter is the world's most powerful woman – by a long way. Not a bad result for a girl who started her career as a Mafia putana."

I fiddled with my fish for a while as I took in the ramifications of everything he was telling me.

"So what about Chuck?"

"Jo-Jo fell in love with Chuck. I'm sure Lillian would have liked to get rid of him, but he was just a simple farm boy. He had nothing to lose. If someone has nothing to lose then it is pretty hard to threaten them. Maybe Jo-Jo simply refused to be dissuaded. She is also a powerful personality, even if she lacks that final core of steel that Lillian has."

"Did you go to their wedding?"

"Nobody went to the wedding, not even their parents. Jo-Jo wrote me a long letter afterwards, telling me she wished I could have been there, but they couldn't let anyone know about it till it was done. She told everyone else that it was to avoid the media attention, but she told me that it was because she didn't want Lillian trying to put a stop to it."

"But they all seemed to get on well at the house."

"Maybe Lillian came to see the usefulness of an all-American father for her grandkids – plus he was a really good looking guy."

"Good breeding stock," I said, remembering my conversation with Chuck.

"As you say," he allowed himself a smile. "My guess is she decided to play a long game, waiting until she had something to leverage him with, something that he would want to protect, maintaining her relationship with Jo-Jo, making herself indispensable to the kids. Maybe she always knew that one day they would be useful as bait."

I looked up from my plate, knife and fork in the air. "Bette and Harvey?"

"What decent, upstanding man wouldn't give his own life to save his children?"

"Chuck was certainly a decent man."

"But would a woman married to a flaky farm boy like Chuck stand as good a chance of being voted president as a beautiful young widow with two photogenic kids who have tragically lost their father – and a great back story?"

"You think she arranged for the shooter to be on the school roof, knowing that Chuck would make himself an easy target and it would not look like he had been the real target?"

Gianni shrugged, as if he was satisfied his work was now done, and went back to his lamb roulade. Two days later he would be dead.

28

That evening I showed the love letters to Caroline and told her the gist of Gianni's story.

"If I am going to publish my diary of the whole business," I said, "then I would need to include this meeting."

She nodded her agreement. "But you can't include these letters, not without Jo-Jo's permission, and I doubt she would give that in her current position. If you waited until she is no longer in office ...."

"I don't think we should wait. I think it is a story that should be told now, while it's still relevant. The world should know if organised crime has managed to infiltrate its tentacles into the White House. Maybe the letters can be published later, or go to some museum or something."

"It is not unusual for mobsters to get into power," she pointed out.

"That doesn't mean it's right or that we should turn a blind eye."

"No, I agree. Giles will never publish this story though. His lawyers will never allow it."

"I know. Would you publish it?"

She thought for a second. "Yes," she said. "I would publish it."

"Even though lawyers would tell you not to?"

"Once the story is out there I can't see what they would gain by suing. They would just be adding more fuel to the fire if they did that because the press would cover every second of any courtroom drama. More likely they would just ignore it; try to make it look like it is such a ridiculous idea they are not even going to dignify it with a reaction."

So that, dear reader, is how this book came to be in your hands today. It is all due to the courage of my wife, whose idea the whole thing was in the first place. And if you should hear that I have met with any kind of fatal accident, you will know where to go with your questions.

Acknowledgements

Every book is a team effort and the team at RedDoor are the people who make things happen and make the publishing process enjoyable. Every author's ideas come from the people he or she meets and the stories that they tell. To everyone inside RedDoor and all those outside whose stories and characters I have plundered for this book, many thanks.

Praise for *Secrets of The Italian Gardener*

"... the characters are so **carefully created** and **multi-layered**, and the storyline **so involving** that we are led into contemplating **the banality of evil** and the complexity of the human psyche almost without realising it"

– Vulpes Libris

"Write about what you know – good advice, which Andrew Crofts has wisely followed in this novella, whose narrator is, like the author, a leading ghostwriter. A story of personal tragedy with an **intriguing** glimpse behind the scenes of dictatorial power"

– Mail Online

"This **fast-paced** narrative will have you **gripped** from start to finish"

– The Lady

"Robert Harris meets Paulo Coelho in a **thoughtful**, **intelligent** story"

– Words-in-Jam

"A contemporary re-casting of Ecclesiastes, this story is about the vanity associated with the **desire for power** and possessions and ultimately about the cycle of birth, growth, death and re-birth"

– Robert Kirby, United Agents

"One of the most **compelling**, **intelligent** and **emotional** books I have read in a long time ... It speaks volumes of the world we live in today and I can't remember ever being this **excited** about a work"

– Wattpad review

Also by Andrew Crofts

Mo, the wealthy dictator of a volatile Middle Eastern country, enlists a ghostwriter to tell his story to the world, enshrining him in history as a glorious ruler. Inside Mo's besieged palace the ghost forms a friendship with a wise and seemingly innocent Italian gardener who slowly reveals that the regime isn't all it appears to be. The ghost discovers the shocking truth of who really holds the power and wealth in the world.

As a violent rebellion threatens all their lives, the ghost is also struggling to cope with a personal secret too painful to bear.

Secrets of the Italian Gardener takes the reader on a heart-pounding journey through the bloody downfall of a doomed tyrant in the company of a young couple struggling to cope with the greatest private tragedy imaginable.

Find out more about
RedDoor Publishing and
sign up to our newsletter
to hear about our **latest
releases**, **author events**,
exciting **competitions**
and more at

reddoorpublishing.com

YOU CAN ALSO FOLLOW US:

 @RedDoorBooks

 RedDoorPublishing

 @RedDoorBooks